For the Love of Ruthie

by

Tenaya E. Jacob

Published by
Satin Romance
An Imprint of Melange Books, LLC
White Bear Lake, MN 55110
www.satinromance.com

For the Love of Ruthie ~ Copyright © 2014 by Tenaya E. Jacob

ISBN: 978-1-68046-020-9

Cover Art by Stephanie Flint

To my mother whose constant love, support and encouragement led me to the completion and successful publication of my first full-length novel.

Chapter One
~ Tony, the Rat ~

Columbus, Ohio

Only a few days till the wedding.

Clarissa Wilford fumbled with her keys to the new condo she and her fiancé Tony would soon occupy. Exhausted after dealing with contentious accountants, insurance representatives, and stodgy hospital executives, she dumped her purse and parcels on the foyer table. The thought of soaking in the spa tub for an hour would be heaven.

The pounding thrum of a guitar dueling with the beat of a drum penetrated her senses. Tony must have forgotten to turn off the stereo. She followed the noise up the curving stairs to the master bedroom. When she reached the threshold, she stopped in shocked silence.

Standing in the doorway to the luxury condo's master bedroom, she couldn't think, speak, or move. Right there, on her new king-sized bed, two naked figures thrashed about, giving the mattress a thorough workout. Gradually her mind accepted what her eyes saw. Her groom-to-be was humping her best friend and maid of honor.

Red-hot fury consumed Clarissa. She took a step forward.

"No!"

An icy chill replaced the heat. She turned on her heel and stumbled, but caught her balance. With an agonized yowl, she fled.

1

Chapter Two
~ The New Neighbor ~

Logan, Ohio, Two years later

"Outside, Ruthie," Clarissa coaxed her small, roly-poly pig as she held open the backdoor to a fenced yard. "Later we'll go for a walk and see what's happening at the old Jenkin place."

She had no idea when or who had built the Jenkin's cabin, but the weathered, hand-hewn logs suggested nineteenth century construction. When old man Jenkin died, the county moved his frail wife Lucy, then in the advanced stage of Alzheimer's, to a nursing home. Clarissa made a mental note to visit her with some flowers in the next few days. The thought of that destructive curse brought a vulnerable feeling to Clarissa and saddened her. The future could be so uncertain.

Curiosity about her new neighbors filled her thoughts. A couple, a widow, or maybe even a retired businessman looking for peace in the country would be fine. Just so long as it wasn't some young punk from the city or a gung-ho hunter. Old man Jenkin had done his share and then some to decimate the local wildlife. The thought of a beautiful deer covered in blood appalled her. All life should be sacred. Guns had no place in civilized society.

Clarissa turned her attention to Ruthie as the pig investigated the yard and then watered a dandelion. With her cute perky ears, she stood no higher than a small dog. Beautiful long eyelashes framed her intelligent brown eyes, and her warm soft snout sensed every interesting odor, especially food. She began to root, her favorite activity, while a busy squirrel gathered acorns from an old oak tree nearby.

2

Amused, Clarissa watched Ruthie sniff the air and eye the critter stuffing its cheek pouches with nuts. The pig raced to the oak at top speed and gobbled acorns like a ravenous vulture. The little squirrel froze in surprise, but recovered at once and nipped the greedy invader on the snout. A loud squeal rent the air.

Clarissa laughed when the startled squirrel flipped its bushy tail in Ruthie's face and scampered pell-mell up the tall oak to a sturdy limb. Safe in the tree, it glared down at her and scolded like an outraged trumpeter swan.

Trying to suppress her laughter at the fuss, Clarissa moved toward her pet. "See, Ruthie, that's what you get for stealing acorns." She reached down to reassure the startled pig.

"Ouch." Something hard bounced off her head. An acorn dropped in front of her and rolled to a stop at her feet.

Gazing up, she glimpsed the angry squirrel chattering away in the tree and dropping acorns with surprising accuracy on her and Ruthie. Its antics amused her, but the acorns hurt.

"You've bothered our little friend. No wonder he wants to chase you away."

Clarissa went inside and returned with the pig's leash and harness. "Come on, Ruthie, too many acorns will make you fat." She dangled the harness in front of Ruthie. "Let's take that walk." It would give the squirrel enough time to harvest the acorns.

Ruthie came at a run, her straight pink tail swishing from side to side. She loved walks almost as much as food. Clarissa slipped the harness over the pig's head, and Ruthie lifted first one dainty hoof into the openings for her front legs and then the other.

With a quick snap, Clarissa fastened the lead to the harness ring and gave a little tug. "Okay, sweetie, let's explore."

The warm sun promised a pleasant day. The early autumn leaves brightened the rolling landscape. Clarissa admired the breathtaking view of the tree-covered hills and valley that sheltered a fascinating variety of wildlife. Early morning and late evening, shy deer grazed. Once, she even glimpsed a red fox. The old picturesque, but vacant log cabin of her nearest neighbor, the Jenkin place, lay out of sight just over the hill.

As the winding country road crested the rise, she saw the For Sale sign on the log cabin had disappeared, and a Sold sign replaced it. Someone had bought the old place. The new owner had plenty of work ahead. Old man Jenkin couldn't be bothered to fix up the place. The trim needed scraping and a coat of paint. The old porch looked downright dangerous with its worn and rickety steps.

"What do you think, Ruthie? Shall we stop by and say hello?"

Ruthie sniffed and tugged forward on her leash. Smiling, Clarissa and Ruthie climbed the two crumbling steps to the sagging porch and walked to the heavy wooden plank door. She gave it several sharp raps.

"Hello? Anyone home?"

No one answered.

"I guess the owner isn't here, Ruthie. We'll stop by another time." Ruthie grunted and followed Clarissa back toward the road.

* * * *

David Claremont stood beside his pickup truck filled with boxes and a red motorcycle. He fumed with irritation as he wondered where his real estate agent was with the keys. The empty road offered no reassurance. Exhausted after working at the free homeless clinic for twenty-four hours straight, David wanted nothing more than a good sleep. He had seen far too many teen suicides and deaths from gunshot wounds. When he couldn't save Sam, the boy he mentored as a Big Brother, from a gunshot wound to the head, he put in his notice. His eyes teared up.

That last twenty-four hour shift had left him worn out physically, but the memory of Sam would scar him for a lifetime. Jasper, his orange cat, paws splayed on the driver side window, mewed in protest.

"Okay, okay, I get the message." He opened the truck door, and Jasper jumped out. The cat licked his paws and then twined around David's ankles.

"All right, Jazz." He tried again to reach the real estate lady by cell phone, but no signal showed. "We'll get in soon even if I have to break a window." Jasper purred and rubbed up against his leg.

After standing around for a while, David looked for a branch, a large stone, or anything to break a window—not a favorable start in a new home. He hefted a heavy broken limb and stalked to the nearest window. He pulled back his arm, ready to smash the glass.

A Lexus roared into the drive and pulled up in a cloud of dust. A woman in a tight red suit dashed toward him.

"I'm so sorry," Donna Gilead, the realtor, gasped. "I'm running late. I got caught up with a client and then hit construction on the way here."

She handed him a set of keys. Dressed in a straight skirt and business jacket, her average height and tight clothes emphasized her chubbiness. She wore too much makeup, which made her look like a cross between a hooker and a middle-aged woman trying to look younger. Well, he certainly had the middle-aged part right.

"Thanks." David clutched the keys and wished her gone. "I've looked forward to checking out my new place."

"I've switched over the electricity for you. After you get settled a bit, why don't you join me this Friday for the festival in the town square? It would give you a chance to meet others and see the town at its best. I could introduce you to a few of the townspeople and some of your new neighbors." Donna waited with a hopeful smile.

"Uh, maybe," he said. "I'll think about it and get back to you."

He was too tired for local gossip or even a friendly chat. He wanted to unload the truck and get some sleep.

"Great!" Donna gave him a broad smile, revealing all her teeth. "Just make sure you let me know before Friday. Well, I'll leave you to it. I have a client waiting to see a house." She got in her car and drove away, leaving him alone at last.

David grabbed a box and headed toward the front door with Jasper trotting at his heels. Once inside, the sunlight illuminated all the dust. The place needed a thorough cleaning and a few repairs. Later, he told himself, much later.

After another hour, he finished unloading the truck and filled Jasper's dishes with food and water. Exhausted, David could do no more. He tumbled onto the dusty moth-eaten couch and closed his eyes.

Bang, bang.

"What the…?" David raised his head and opened one eye.

Bang! Bang! The pounding came again, louder.

Shaking his head, he struggled to his feet. Someone at the door? What now?

Stumbling forward, he yanked open the door. "Yes?" He yawned and stretched. "What?"

He glared at the youngish, wiry man dressed in a windbreaker and worn jeans. The man's old Buick sat next to his truck.

"Hi, neighbor, I'm Jimmy Johnson, the local newspaper carrier." He held out his hand, which David ignored. "Since you're new to the area, I'm sure you can use a subscription to the *Logan Gazette*. Lots of stuff to help you get settled. Here's a copy of today's paper." He thrust a rolled paper at David.

"I don't read papers." David pushed the paper back at him and yawned. Why couldn't everyone just leave him alone?

"Okay, but if you change your mind, here's my card; just call me. Say, that's a nice bike you got there." Jimmy eyed David's large red Honda motorcycle sitting in the driveway. "Lots of pretty country around here to ride it."

"Yeah, uh, thanks." David started to close the door.

"You hunt, man?" Jimmy asked.

"What?" David stared at him unable to make the connection.

"Hunt, you know, like deer. We got lots of deer around here. Old man Jenkin, he'd bag his quota and then some every year. The ranger kept citing him and threatened to take his guns."

"Oh?" David raised one eyebrow.

"Yeah, if you'd like a hunting buddy, let me know. Always works better with two or more to track a wounded animal." Jimmy gave him a hopeful look.

"Yeah, I'm dead tired right now. We can talk about hunting later." David shut the door and staggered back to the couch.

"See you soon," Jimmy called through the closed door.

David barely heard the sound of the car as it roared away. He collapsed and dozed off into a peaceful slumber.

* * * *

After supper, Clarissa reached for Ruthie's leash. "Okay, I guess it's time for our walk. Why don't we try our new neighbor's house again and see if anyone's home? Maybe a nice newlywed couple or an older woman bought it. I'd like to have someone to visit close to home every now and then. Just so we don't get someone like old man Jenkin."

Ruthie snorted and rubbed against Clarissa's leg. Clarissa grabbed a small basket of fruit she had sitting on her kitchen table to take as a welcome gift for her new neighbor and headed out the front door. Ruthie trotted close by her side. They soon reached the cabin.

A red pickup truck parked in the cabin's driveway signified someone was home. A red motorcycle sat next to the truck. Practical transportation given the price of gas, but did that mean a red-necked yokel? Shuddering at that thought, she hoped not.

Clarissa took care negotiating the slanting steps and the gaping boards of the porch. She rapped at the plank door of the cabin. No one answered, so she knocked again, this time louder.

A tall, broad-shouldered man yanked open the door and glared at her. A large, orange fur ball that resembled a Halloween cat arched its back. It hissed at Ruthie with its fur standing on end.

"Wee, wee..." Ruthie squealed and hid behind Clarissa.

The cat advanced on stiff legs, a growl rising in the back of its throat.

Dumbfounded, Clarissa stared at it. "It...it won't bite, will it?"

She glanced from the irate cat to the glowering man. He skewered her and Ruthie with an icy gaze. She clutched the basket of fruit to her chest.

"Uh, hello, welcome to the neighborhood. I brought you some fruit. I'm your next-door neighbor, Clarissa Wilford, and this is Ruthie. We live just down the road at the top of that hill." She pointed to the hill she had just walked up with her left hand.

"Oh?" The man pinned her with eyes filled with anger. "Neighbor?" His narrow eyes reflected suspicion.

His scroungy, two-day growth of beard reminded her of old man Jenkin. At least his flannel shirt had no tears. Worn jeans encased a sturdy pair of legs. His cold green eyes offered no more welcome than his belligerent cat.

Clarissa kept her distance. Determined to be friendly, she tried again. "Uh, if you have any questions about the area, you can call on me anytime." She waited, uncertain how he would respond.

"What are you selling?" the man snapped.

"Nothing, I'm just a neighbor stopping by to welcome you to the area." She shifted from foot to foot in the doorway.

"Forget it. Go away."

"I only wanted to welcome you. Here's a fruit basket." She shoved the fruit into his hands and spun on her heel.

In her haste to leave, she failed to notice Ruthie between her legs, and she stumbled on the porch steps. Unbalanced, she tripped and pitched face forward down the rickety steps. She landed on her hands and knees in the grass. Thank heaven she'd worn her jeans.

"You okay, lady?" He approached her to offer help.

Ruthie nudged her with her soft pink snout. Clarissa shook her head and scrambled to her feet. The man gazed at her with amusement. She feared he might burst out laughing at any moment, compounding her humiliation.

"No, thank you. I'm fine." She spat the words at him and stalked away with Ruthie fast on her heels. "What an awful, self-centered man."

To think he had the audacity to look amused by her fall. Clarissa fumed, her face flushed with anger, while tears of embarrassment stung her eyes.

Ruthie trotted alongside her as she set a brisk pace down the road toward home. It appeared this new neighbor would turn out to be another old man Jenkin. More's the pity.

"Anti-social, bad-mannered, and...dirty. We won't bother him again. What do you think, Ruthie?" Ruthie grunted all four legs almost a blur beside Clarissa.

"And that awful monster cat of his. We don't want neighbors like that."

Ruthie snorted as if in agreement.

Chapter Three
~ The Savvy Investor ~

The bright morning sun filtered through the lace curtains into Clarissa's bedroom. The light blue of the walls echoed the sky, and the sunbeam illuminated the yellow loveseat under the window where she sometimes read. It also touched the big oak desk in the corner she had refinished only last month.

Opening one eye, she glanced at her clock. Six fifty-five. Only five minutes until her alarm clock would ring. She might as well get up. She stretched, shut-off her alarm, and then slipped her bare feet into her fuzzy pink pig slippers.

Ruthie stirred as Clarissa slid out of bed and then ambled after her. Yawning, Clarissa padded to the back door to let Ruthie out to do her business and sighed in relief not to see the squirrel about.

Today, she planned to visit old man Jenkin's wife Lucy in the nursing home. Then she would stop by the Logan Antique Mall and check on her rental space. Her display needed sprucing up to attract more customers. Sales had declined lately, probably due to higher gas and grocery prices.

Prices for everything had risen, except for people's incomes. Maybe if she added some new pieces for Halloween she could attract new sales. Local folks hereabouts celebrated Halloween with gusto, and some tourists, glad for autumn's arrival, drove into the country to enjoy the color of the fall leaves. Some of them stopped at the antique mall and often bought something.

"Come, Ruthie, it's time for our morning stroll." She grabbed the pig's lead and harness from a hook by the door, and they headed into the fresh morning air.

Outside, Clarissa led Ruthie down the long driveway to the gravel road for a short half-mile walk up and back down the hill past old man Jenkin's place. She hoped a little sleep had cleared the nasty new owner's brain.

"We won't knock on his door again."

"Humph, humph," Ruthie gazed up at Clarissa with her expressive brown eyes as if to say *I agree.*

"It's going to be a beautiful day, Ruthie." She bent down and patted her pig. Ruthie responded as Clarissa scratched behind her perky ear and rubbed against Clarissa's leg.

"We'd better get back so I can finish things and go to town." She tugged on Ruthie's leash, but the little pig didn't budge. "Come on, Ruthie, what is it, girl?"

She looked around and glimpsed something like a flash of orange in the brush staring at Ruthie. A fox? No, not that large. Its arched back signaled a possible attack. It hissed and growled. No wonder Ruthie wouldn't move. Still only two, Ruthie acted like a young piglet, and any loud noise frightened her. She hid behind Clarissa and quivered.

"It's that darn cat, isn't it?" Clarissa stamped her foot and waved her arms at the cat lurking in the roadside bushes. "Scat, go on, *Get!"*

The cat glared at her and Ruthie, but didn't move.

"Come on, Ruthie." Clarissa tugged harder. At last, the little pig followed her with reluctant steps while looking back with a cautious eye at the cat.

* * * *

David yawned as he stood in front of his stove and scrambled some eggs and fried a couple of sausage links. He had risen a bit late today. The sizzling sausage made his mouth water in anticipation. He speculated over what his nosy new neighbor and her pet pig were doing.

"Here, kitty, kitty. Jasper," he called out the backdoor and looked around. "Where are you, cat?"

Jasper came running, ready for breakfast. A pet door would give Jasper access, David thought. He'd have to stop at the hardware store and see what they had. He put cat food in Jasper's bowl, and Jazz ate it all. He purred like a well-tuned engine as David sat down to his own breakfast.

Even though he'd been dead-tired and half-asleep yesterday, the memory remained of a beautiful, shapely brunette with shoulder-length brown hair and piercing green eyes accompanied by a plump, little pink pig. He'd never seen a pig so small before. An interesting choice for a pet. The little pig behaved well and looked appealing. He laughed as he wondered whether the woman also had a Charlotte like the spider in *Charlotte's Web*.

Too bad the woman had pried into his business. Having her for a neighbor could cause trouble. He didn't want to have anyone find out about Sam. The memory of the boy's recent death still pained him. However, at least he ought to apologize for his rudeness.

With breakfast finished and the dishes done, David walked with Jasper outside to check out his new surroundings. Hills and trees stretched as far as he could see with wide-open spaces and only a few scattered houses on the horizon. The houses sat far apart, giving the appearance of being alone, one of the reasons the area attracted him.

As he and Jasper strolled a little way down the road, he glimpsed a small group of five well-fed deer grazing by the edge of the woods. He counted four doe and one buck. David stared at them with surprise as they continued to graze. When he and Jasper neared the herd, the deer ran off, white tails high.

"We'll be eating venison this year, Jazz." The cat purred as he rubbed up against David's leg.

Jimmy, the newspaper guy, had mentioned hunting. He probably knew all the good spots. David would call him sometime to do a bit of hunting and learn the lay of the land.

When he reached the bend in the road, he savored the beautiful view of his cabin nestled in front of rolling green hills. He'd made the right decision to buy it and leave the clutter, crime, and clamor of the city behind. At least any gunshot wounds here would come from accidents and not from robberies or revenge killings. No young boys killed by thugs and drug dealers here.

He would never raise any future family he might have in the big city. Sam had only been fourteen. How could life be so cruel?

"We're going to like it here just fine, Jazz." He tried to erase the images of the dead teen from his mind.

Jasper sounded like a small airplane as David stroked him and scratched under his chin.

* * * *

Following their morning walk, Ruthie sat and watched as Clarissa opened the fridge to look for fruit and a few veggies for her pig, and milk for her own cereal. She dropped the fruit and veggies in Ruthie's dish along with the usual pig-food pellets. After giving Ruthie fresh water, she sat down with a bowl of Raisin Bran, a cup of tea, and the morning paper. The only news of note was a piece on the Friday evening celebration hosted by local merchants. She wondered if the antique mall would be open, but it sat at north of town and was a mile or two from the downtown area.

After breakfast, Clarissa headed to the sunny room to the left of the living room where she kept her glassware. The sunlight sparkled on her growing collection. She had acquired pieces from a variety of thrift stores, Internet purchases, and the occasional yard sale. People in the area had collected a lot of Ohio glassware over the years and, in these difficult times, sold off odd pieces. Often the original purchaser had died, and the heirs had no idea of the value of such items. They only wanted to get rid of what they considered clutter.

She selected a few attractive pieces from the shelves that lined the walls and formed rows through the center of the small room. She checked to ensure they had tags with a description, inventory number, and a price. Finally, she packed them in a cardboard box to take to the antique mall. Finished, she headed for the front door with the box.

Once at the Logan Antique Mall, Clarissa began changing her display. The mall wasn't small, but not large either. On the outside porch, an assortment of old antiques such as baskets, wooden and metal chairs, ceramics, cheap glassware, and lamps attracted buyers. Inside, the checkout counter sat just beyond the entrance with vertical rows of booths rising on either side. Each booth contained a mixture of mostly small items, but more expensive collectables, jewelry, glassware, and some clothing.

Clarissa's space lay to the left of the checkout at the beginning of the last aisle toward the back of the store. She had leased a space six feet wide and about five feet long. Bookcases partitioned it off from the adjoining spaces and offered plenty of shelves. A glass showcase occupied the front section of her booth.

Various pieces of Ohio and the surrounding states' collectible glassware filled the shelves and a variety of table runners provided more color and a decorative touch. She focused on achieving contrast through strategic placement by color and shape. The showcase featured the newest pieces, often with a holiday theme. Before she realized it, several hours had passed and her stomach growled.

Just then, a tall man with sparkling blue eyes and a gorgeous smile approached her. He held one of her pieces. A stylist had sculpted his glistening sandy hair in a short cut with plenty of waves. She bet he had no trouble with women—his type never did.

"Is this bowl for sale or just for display?" He held out the shallow, star-shaped, red piece. "I couldn't find the price."

Clarissa took it and examined the bottom. "It must have fallen off. Let me check my inventory sheet a moment and I can tell you."

She flipped through her notebook until she came across the piece. "It's a Viking Epic dish. The red is an unusual and expensive color to make. It requires gold. This piece is forty-five dollars."

"Thanks," he replied. "I'm Brent Soulder. He flashed that soul-melting smile again.

"Say, why don't you join me for a cup of coffee and we can discuss this piece." He gazed at her with that gorgeous smile and reclaimed the bowl.

His hand brushed hers and sent sparks along her nerves. Lost in those ocean-blue eyes and captivated by his ravishing smile, Clarissa considered his invitation. It wouldn't hurt to have a cup of coffee. She needed a break anyway.

"Okay. I'm ready to wrap things up here, and tea would be heaven."

Brent's broad smile showcased his perfect white teeth. He paid for his purchase at the checkout counter.

They walked side-by-side to the Dutch Restaurant next door. Inside the cozy seating area, he purchased a cup of coffee and another of tea, along with two slices of fresh fruit pie.

Clarissa watched him from a square table for two near the windows. The place was empty. No other customers had arrived yet.

He offered her a choice of blackberry or Dutch apple pie. She took the apple. The homemade pies drew many customers all year round. People loved Amish and Mennonite baked goods

As Brent sipped his coffee, he focused an intense gaze on her. "I'm a financial adviser myself," he said. "What about you, that is, besides glassware?"

She pondered a minute, not sure she wanted to discuss her business with a stranger, no matter how attractive he looked. Tony had made her cautious about men.

"I'm a medical billing consultant for a few local doctors' offices."

"Oh? You're an independent businesswoman then?" He raised an expressive eyebrow.

"Yes, I have been for the past two years. Before that, I worked for the local hospital here in Logan." Clarissa focused on her steaming tea.

"You do much trading?"

"Trading? You mean in glassware?"

Brent laughed. "No, trading as in investing. It's a good way to make your money work for you."

"I have a few investments," Clarissa said, not liking the question. "With all the market turmoil of late, I'm unwilling to do more."

"Yeah, I know what you mean." He sighed. "Still, there are opportunities if you know where to look. I could give you some suggestions. I build for the future. You have to protect yourself and your investments these days. It takes an expert to keep from losing big."

She gazed at him, disappointed his interest appeared to be finding a new customer. "I'm doing fine. Besides, I already own a house and can't think of anything more I need."

"You forgot to mention your glassware." Brent sipped his coffee with amused eyes.

Clarissa blinked, wondering where he was heading. "What about it?"

"Surely you make money from it or you wouldn't waste your time."

"Well, I make a little, but without my billing work, I couldn't survive on the profit from glassware sales. I love beautiful things, and the glass is part of the area's history." If he wanted a client he'd best look elsewhere.

"I could probably help you double your money. I suspect you wouldn't mind building your retirement income. Of course, an attractive woman like you could marry a well-to-do man."

"Humph," Clarissa snorted. "I don't have to depend on someone else to support me. I'm more than able to take care of myself."

"You're not a man-hater, are you?" He eyed her as if amused.

"Look, all I said was I can manage my resources quite well, thank you."

"Ooh, I've hit a sore spot." He looked thoughtful and sipped his coffee. "Maybe I should start again. Let's forget about money and futures. How about having dinner Friday night?" Brent raised an eyebrow at her in challenge.

"Um, I don't know." She hesitated, not at all certain about him or his motives. "We've only just met."

"True, but I'd like to change that. Besides, it would be fun. I know a restaurant in Logan only the locals know about. They serve a marvelous rack of ribs. What do you say we take a chance to get better acquainted? I'm a nice guy, really." He flashed that hundred-watt smile at her again.

"I suppose it wouldn't do any harm."

Having dinner out would be nice. She didn't do that often. She handed him her business card, and without hesitation he gave her his.

She'd given him her telephone number and e-mail address if he changed his mind. She hadn't had a date since she broke up with Tony, and Brent was eye candy. It wouldn't hurt to be seen with him.

"Finding my place can be a little difficult," Clarissa said. "We'd better meet here in front of the antique mall."

"Okay, see you here at six on Friday then." Brent's lips brushed the back of her hand for good measure.

She couldn't help the deep blush on her cheeks. Would he prove to be a man she could spend time with and enjoy his company, or would he turn out to be a jerk like Tony.

* * * *

Sitting on her back porch with Ruthie that evening, Clarissa stared mesmerized by the sunset with its gorgeous array of colors. The brilliance faded in the sky, leaving a soft afterglow like watercolors. She smiled in contentment and remembered her childhood in the big city of Columbus, Ohio. She always hated all the hustle and bustle of people and traffic, most of all the traffic. Tall buildings and houses with hardly any trees to soften the view. She'd begun feel caged and hemmed in by it all until she moved to Logan.

Her mother always told her to develop herself through education and setting goals. She'd often dreamed of living in a quaint little house in the country. She'd given that up for a while with Tony. Now, having fled to the country, she'd achieved her dream.

With pride, she reflected back on how, with hard work and perseverance, she'd obtained her bachelor's degree in medical billing. It took an additional two years after that to gain sufficient experience to allow her to work from home as an independent contractor. Several more years passed before she earned a reasonable living for herself and Ruthie.

Comfortably settled now, she wanted a future with a husband and maybe even a child or two. Her memories included a great childhood exploring the local creek and the nearby golf course. She and her brother Cliff recovered lost golf balls and sold them to the golfers for spending money. Yes, she wanted a family like the one in which she'd grown up.

Ruthie nudged her leg, seeking attention. Clarissa smiled and reached down to rub the pig's soft ears. Her Aunt Mary had given Ruthie to her as a birthday present. In the beginning, she didn't know what to say or how to act, but after the first few weeks with Ruthie, she came to realize how much the little pig enriched her life. This adorable pot-bellied pig behaved better than any dog Clarissa had ever known. She had never met such an intelligent animal before, and could no longer imagine a single day without Ruthie by her side.

The afterglow faded to a darkening sky, and a few stars popped up as it continued to grow darker. The mild air invited her to stay a bit longer. Then, an eerie howl filled the air as a dark shape emerged from the trees. Ruthie squealed and hid behind Clarissa. Her little legs shook and her body trembled.

The black blur crept into the backyard. Was it a dog? Folks dropped off dogs in the country, and sometimes they formed packs. Clarissa once had to call the animal control office to round up a pack of feral dogs. She had worried they would attack Ruthie or even her.

Now, certain the invader represented a dog, Clarissa scrambled to scoop up Ruthie in her arms.

She dashed inside and slammed the door behind her. Setting Ruthie down, she peered out the living room window. Sure enough, the dog sniffed around the yard and came closer to the porch.

Chapter Four
~ The Town Gossip ~

Clarissa ran into the kitchen and rummaged through her cabinets. With a pan in each hand, she ran to the back door, yanked it open, and banged the pans together.

Cling, Clang, Bang!

The skinny wild dog still looked menacing with its size and wolf-like appearance. Startled by the sound of the pans banging, it ran off into the woods.

"It's okay, Ruthie, that wild dog isn't going to get you." She collapsed on her couch and cuddled Ruthie in her arms, stroking her head gently and cooing to the frightened pig. "Everything's okay." She only hoped that dog stayed away and had no friends nearby.

Anxious to soothe Ruthie and her own fears, she chose an evening movie to watch from her DVD collection. They both liked *Babe*. She poured a half-glass of merlot wine and made popcorn for the movie.

They always watched movies in her bedroom. There, Ruthie settled into her wicker basket with a large pillow next to Clarissa's queen-sized canopy bed. Clarissa changed into her nightgown and popped the DVD into the player.

As she snuggled into her comfortable bed, her thoughts turned to Brent at the antique mall and their date Friday. He had distinct possibilities. She'd know more about those possibilities after they had dinner together. On the other hand, his questions about her finances annoyed her. They were much too personal a thing to ask this soon. For now, she'd give him the benefit of the doubt. Those hunky looks of his and his kiss on the hand had made her heart do flip-flops.

While hitting the play button on the DVD remote, she reached down with her other hand to pat Ruthie. Munching on popcorn and sipping wine, she tossed a few kernels at a time to Ruthie, mindful not to overdo it. When the movie ended, she turned out the light and settled down to sleep.

"Goodnight, Ruthie, I'll see you in the morning." Ruthie gave a contented grunt.

* * * *

In Dr. Jennings's office at nine Monday morning, David reviewed patient records as he waited for his first appointment to arrive. On this, his first day at Dr. Jennings's Family Physicians Practice, the small but modern looking doctor's office impressed him. As soon as he entered, he'd noticed the clean, light-green walls with green leafy borders. Restful pictures of hills, streams, and meadows lined them.

The waiting area, just to the left of the entrance, contained padded chairs and a coffee table in the center. The table held a wide selection of magazines for the adults, while a children's play area, set in one corner, provided toys and a playhouse. The friendlier environment offered more welcome than the cold, sterile atmosphere at the big city hospital he came from. There, white barren walls reflected overhead fluorescents, and medical journals with a few drug company publications replaced family magazines.

Here, Geneva, the matronly receptionist, greeted patients and directed them to the waiting area. A middle-aged motherly type with auburn hair graying around her temples, she wore wire-framed granny glasses. The lines around her mouth and eyes made him think she smiled a lot.

As David read the appointment list, to his surprise, he came across Jimmy Johnson's name. The newspaper guy who had stopped by the other day? Interesting. He grabbed the clipboard from the outside chart holder on the door of the first examination room. Glancing over the nurse's notes on vital signs and symptoms reported by the patient, he entered the room.

David noticed the décor resembled the waiting room, only smaller, with fewer magazines and no toys. The examination table sat in the middle and a small counter lined the far wall with a chair. A blue-eyed, sandy-haired little boy of about six fidgeted on the examination table. Jimmy, the newspaperman, sat in a chair to the right of the table.

Jimmy smiled as David held out his hand and greeted him. "Hey, how's it goin'?" He shook David's hand.

"Not bad, I'm sorry I was a little short with you when we met the other day. You caught me after a long couple days at work, and I was exhausted."

"I understand, no problem, I get to be a real bear when I'm tired." Jimmy smiled with friendly warmth.

"I wanted to tell you I went out early this morning to get a feel for the area around my cabin and saw five deer grazing near the woods—several doe and one buck. They looked well fed." David moved around the small desk and sat in the doctor's chair behind it. A laptop computer occupied the center of the work surface. At least he didn't have to write his notes in longhand.

"Really?" Jimmy looked pleased. "We'll have to get together sometime this hunting season and get us a few. I've been all over the old Jenkin place. The old man and me, we bagged a few every year."

"Sounds like a plan." David nodded and turned to the boy. "Yours?"

"Yep, this is Jimmy Junior. He has a bellyache." Jimmy frowned. "His momma sez bring him an' have 'im checked out. She sez there's some bug goin' round."

"Is anyone else in your household sick?"

"No. Why?"

"Sometimes when one person has an illness, it spreads. However, I don't think that's the case here. Well, let's have a look-see and find out what we can." David reached for his stethoscope and turned toward little Jimmy. "This won't hurt a bit, son; I'm just going to listen to your tummy and feel for anything unusual for a minute. See if it growls." Placing it on the boy's abdomen, he grinned at him, and the boy grinned back.

Little Jimmy tried to hold still for David as he listened and palpitated his abdomen, but couldn't help squirming after a few seconds. "Did it growl?"

"A bit, want to listen?"

"Gee, can I?"

"Sure." David held the ear plugs close to the boy's ears. "Did you hear it?"

The blue eyes widened. "Yeah, thanks. Is that my tummy making them funny noises?"

"Yup, it is. Everyone's tummy makes gurgling and bubbling noises. Now let's listen to your heart and lungs a minute." David moved his stethoscope to the boy's chest and asked him to breathe in and out slowly.

After a few breaths, he removed the instrument from boy's chest and keyed in some notes onto his computer. "Everything looks pretty normal. What has he eaten in the last twenty-four hours? Has he had any other symptoms like nausea or diarrhea?"

"Um, I think he had a bowl of cereal this mornin' and spaghetti last night," Jimmy responded. "I'm not sure what else he had to eat, and he hasn't fussed about any other problems."

David smiled at the boy. "Jimmy, have you eaten anything else besides cereal and spaghetti?"

"Um, well…" Little Jimmy hesitated. "I had some candy yesterday I sneaked when momma weren't lookin'." He hung his head and looked sideways at Jimmy. "Um…lots of candy."

Understanding dawned on both David and big Jimmy's faces.

"I see." David turned to address little Jimmy's father. "I suspect too much candy may be the reason for this visit today. For now, just keep an eye on him, give him plenty of liquids, and give him some Pepto-Bismol. Watch too much sugary stuff and no soda pop," David advised. "Do you have Pepto-Bismol in your medicine cabinet at home?

"Uh, yeah, I think so," Jimmy replied. "Is that the pink stuff?"

"Yes. Give him some, and if his stomachache gets worse or is still bothering him tomorrow, bring him back." David patted little Jimmy on the leg. "All done, sport, you can go home now. Don't get into any more candy without your mom or dad's permission, okay."

The boy gave David a weak grin and slowly climbed down from the examining table.

"Don't worry, he should be feeling much better by tomorrow," David reassured Jimmy who still looked a bit worried.

"Thanks for everythin', Doc. You need ta let me show ya the best huntin' spots sometime soon."

"Sure, how about this weekend?"

Jimmy looked pleasantly surprised. "Okay, there're lots of wild turkeys around, and I'm sure we can bag us a couple. How 'bout I come round your place at six Saturday morning?"

"Sure, that'll work. I'll see you then." David patted Jimmy on the back to send him on his way.

He watched father and son walk across the parking lot to the beat-up old Buick. To David, Jimmy came across as a decent guy. Maybe they'd become good friends and hunting pals. He turned and headed toward the receptionist to consult with her on billing.

"Geneva, what's the standard charge for an office visit?"

"Oh, uh, it's forty dollars plus the cost of supplies," she answered.

"Sir?" She hesitated a moment. "Um, we usually don't charge Jimmy for standard visits. He brings us fresh eggs, produce, and preserves as payment. In fact, he left you this jar of strawberry preserves his wife made."

"Oh?" David raised a brow. "Why?"

Just then, Doctor Jennings joined them. A tall, thin, elderly man with gray hair, with a neatly trimmed mustache and beard, he reminded David of a distinguished professor he'd once had. He looked more like someone's grandfather than a doctor. No suit and tie, just slacks and a nice button-down shirt. Rather casual for a doctor. In fact, only the white lab coat he wore signified *doctor*.

"Hello, David, how are you settling into small-town life?"

"Very well, thank you. It's a pleasant change from the fast-paced hospital life in the city. I'm glad to see you. Geneva was just telling me about the pro-bono work with patients like Jimmy Johnson."

"Yes, we have a few others like that. Jimmy has been coming here since he was a boy; in fact, I delivered him. We all know his finances aren't the best so we give him a break for routine visits." Dr. Jennings smiled.

"Jimmy's led a hard life," Geneva added. "His childhood was difficult. His mother died from cancer, and his father from a heart attack. He works hard taking care of his wife and three kids on a small farm."

She sighed and exchanged a glance with Doctor Jennings. "Jimmy was just eighteen when his dad died and left him the farm. Dr. Jennings believes binge drinking may have led to his father's heart attack." Geneva frowned and looked at her desk.

David nodded with understanding. "Oh, I see. We had a free clinic at the Riverside Hospital in Columbus. It was always filled with uninsured patients. It's a sad world we live in today where people can't afford health insurance. I hope this new law helps."

He looked around. "Speaking of billing, where are those people? I don't believe I've met them yet."

"Well, that's because Clarissa works at home. She only stops in about once or twice a week to collect patient visit information." Geneva organized some papers on her desk.

David stared at her. "Did you say Clarissa?" A vision of an angry brunette with a little pink pig came to mind.

"Miss Wilford's been doing all our medical billing for the last two years. Do you know her?" Geneva looked at David, curiosity foremost.

"I think we met the other day. She's my next-door neighbor." David laughed at the mental picture of his irate neighbor and her plump pig.

"Logan's a small town, and everybody knows everybody else. Most are friendly and you'll have no trouble talking with them. They know we need another doctor." She grinned at him.

"Yeah, so I gathered. Haven't seen much of the town yet."

"Too bad the central business district has taken such a hard hit with some of the stores closing, but we always have busy summers and falls with all the tourists hereabouts. With the boating accidents and fishhooks, we get our share. Then, too, some city boys always manage to turn over one of the canoes. Once hunting season starts, we get some careless folks who don't pay attention. We almost always have some man or boy shoot himself by accident. You won't have to worry about patients."

"Guess I'd better get ready for that next patient then."

* * * *

Clarissa hurried into Dr. Jennings office to collect the weekly patient billing data. A handsome young man stood talking with Geneva and Dr.

Jennings. The new doctor?

She nearly tripped over the rug as she approached Geneva and struggled to regain her composure. When she focused on the man, he looked at her as if he saw something funny about her.

What a klutz. How could she be so clumsy as to trip over her own two feet? Why did the man smile at her like the Cheshire cat from *Alice in Wonderland?*

"To what do I owe this pleasure?" The doctor grinned at Clarissa with a sparkle in his green eyes.

"Oh, um, I'm Clarissa Wilford, and I've come to collect the new patient charts," she responded with a puzzled look on her face. "I do the patient accounts and the medical billing for Dr. Jennings's practice."

"Clarissa, this is Doctor David Claremont, recently from Columbus." Dr. Jennings motioned toward the man. "He's joined the practice and will take over for me when I retire."

"Oh, that's awhile yet." She stared at the new doctor, her brows creased. "You look familiar."

"We met the other day," Doctor Claremont said. "I'm afraid I was a bit rude from lack of sleep at the time."

Realization dawned on her. He was that nasty man with the aggressive orange cat, but he'd had a beard and dressed like a bum. "I...I had no idea you were a doctor."

"Perhaps you two would like a few moments to get acquainted." Geneva gave them an amused look.

"No, no, that's okay," Clarissa stammered. "I really have to go. I have a lot of work to do this afternoon." She accepted the papers from Geneva and prepared to leave.

"Me, too," Dr. Claremont responded. "I have more patients waiting. Perhaps we can talk some more another time, Miss Wilford." He grasped her hand to shake it.

An invigorating chill invaded her body and rendered her paralyzed for one brief moment. Had he felt it, too? Clarissa trembled and nodded at David as he stood for a moment and then walked off toward the next examination room. Why did a man she found abrasive make her insides turn to jelly? What was wrong with her?

* * * *

As David finished with his last patient, he made some final notes on his laptop and shut it down for the day.

"See you tomorrow," he called to Geneva and Dr. Jennings as he headed for his car.

"See you," they responded with a wave.

On his way home, David stopped by the real estate office to sign some last-minute papers on his newly purchased home. As soon as he entered, a wave of some strong perfume engulfed him. He never understood why some women used such heavy scents. It would irritate people with allergies.

The realtor, Mrs. Gilead, sat at a metal desk next to the large front window and looked up as he entered. She welcomed him with a big smile. A young man built like a wrestler with a scar on his right cheekbone was working on repairing a desk. Looking at him brought David too many bad memories of the Columbus emergency room. An uncomfortable, creepy feeling settled over him.

The white office walls had a few pictures of homes and farms for sale, with the rest of the room divided into cubicles. Only the desks had personal pictures and knickknacks. Papers cluttered Mrs. Gilead's desk, a business degree from Hocking College, and lots of poodle memorabilia.

"Doctor Claremont, thank you for stopping by. How's everything going with your new home?"

"Fine, just fine. Mrs. Gilead, I'm here to sign those papers you mentioned."

"Please, call me Donna." She smiled at him and reached into one of her file drawers. She removed a folder with his name on it and handed him several forms to sign.

David scanned them, scrawled his signature at the bottom, and returned them to her.

After filing the papers, she faced him and batted her mascaraed eyelashes. "Have you thought any more about the town festival on Friday? You really ought to come. It'll be fun, and you'll get to meet a number of the townsfolk."

"I'll try," David replied, feeling like a deer in the hunter's sights. "It's just that I often work late at the office on Fridays."

"Well, do try if you can. I'll be looking forward to seeing you at the festival." Her smile implied she had more in mind than just seeing him. Somehow, he felt like dessert.

He reminded himself real estate agents knew most people in town. Maybe he should pick her brain. "I met a fellow named Jimmy Johnson. He stopped by my office today and volunteered to take me hunting with him Saturday morning. Do you know him?"

"Oh, that good-for-nothing Jimmy." Donna grimaced. "Nothing but a penny-ante farmer, he has more kids than he can afford and more land than sense of what to do with it. I've clients who would love to buy it, but Jimmy won't sell. He says it's belonged to his family forever." She released a long sigh.

"Oh?" Her vehement reaction to Jimmy's name surprised David. "He seems like a nice fellow."

"Humph, he's a bum who can barely take care of his family. Not too clean either, if you ask me." She shuddered, and her tone made her distaste clear. "He knocked up his girlfriend at eighteen in high school, but at least he married her. They had two more kids in five years, even though they could barely afford the one. I wonder sometimes if they were ever properly educated about birth control."

"You don't say." Uncomfortable with her tirade, David gave her a weak smile as he debated how to turn off her venom.

"You'd do better to make friends with some of our prominent townsfolk like Mr. Maynard, the mayor, or Ms. Finnegan, the owner of Café Corner. They're well respected in this town and can tell you a lot about our citizens. Why, Mr. Maynard and Ms. Finnegan both grew up around here and graduated from Ohio University together. Mr. Maynard was valedictorian of his high school class, and Ms. Finnegan is the finest cook around," Donna gushed.

"Really?" he said. "Did she graduate with a cooking degree?"

"Oh, heavens no, she has a business degree. She went to school to learn how to run the family restaurant. Ms. Finnegan makes the best pies I've ever had." She licked her lips and rolled her eyes. "You should join me one of these days for a slice of her blueberry pie. It's to die for."

"Sounds like an interesting idea." David tried to remain polite, but had to suppress a laugh at the image of the realtor gobbling pie and then

26

expiring. "I can't remember the last time I had home cooking."

"Call me anytime you're ready, and we'll stop in at the Café for a cup of coffee and a piece of pie."

"Uh sure, thanks for the information. I have to get going now. Likely I'll see you at Friday's festivities." David backed out of the office, glad to breathe air not filled with that awful heavy perfume.

Donna reminded him of the head nurse at the hospital who thought she knew everything and always corrected him. He also suspected the realtor coveted Jimmy's land, so she had a reason to dislike him.

As he drove toward home, he mulled over what she'd said about Jimmy. The way she judged people's success by how much money they earned and what they did for a living didn't sit well with him. Who cared if Jimmy wasn't rich? At least he cared enough about his son to bring him to the doctor. Besides, being well educated and rich wasn't David's idea of what made a person successful.

Jimmy appeared to have other qualities and enjoyed his life, which made him just as successful as any other man. As far as he could tell, Jimmy loved his wife and his kids. He offered friendliness and to share his hunting spots with others. That showed real generosity.

David arrived home tired from his first day at his new office. He wondered what Clarissa was doing right about now. He hadn't said anything, but earlier at the office when they shook hands, a jolt of static electrified him. She definitely triggered his curiosity. He wanted to find out more about her. After all, they would be working together.

He stopped by the local hardware store on the way home and picked up a pet door to install for his cat. When he reached home, Jazz greeted him with his usual loud purr.

"Hey, Jasper, how is my boy doing today?"

Jasper strutted slowly into the room and encircled David's legs. David stoked the orange cat from head to tail, and Jasper's well-tuned-engine purr filled the room. Heading for the kitchen, David grabbed a frozen TV dinner and then popped it in the microwave.

"Here, kitty, kitty… Jasper," he called the cat to the kitchen as he opened a can of cat food and emptied it into a dish. These days the cans had pull-off tops, so he couldn't count on the sound of a can opener, but Jasper knew the click of the can lid just the same and came running.

After dinner, David picked up his violin. He had played it since he was ten and had improved over the years. He pulled out the music he'd used at last year's classical music fundraising event to help kids needing extensive medical treatments. This year, his group hoped to do another to benefit hospice programs for the dying. Jasper leaped up beside him and settled on the couch next to him as he played some Mozart. Soon Jasper snoozed.

Like Jasper, classical music soothed David's spirits. Considering everything, he looked forward to winter evenings in front of the fire with Jasper sleeping by his side. Yes, he congratulated himself on his move to the country. The money might not be as good, but the people, with one or two exceptions like Mrs. Gilead, and the beauty of the countryside more than made up for that.

As he prepared to retire for the evening, he thought about the town festival Mrs. Gilead had mentioned. Should he go? As the town's new doctor, he probably should. As long as Mrs. Gilead kept her hands off him and stopped looking at him like a future husband, he would be fine.

Would Clarissa be there? He wanted an opportunity to make up for his rude behavior toward her on their first encounter and become better acquainted. He had trouble identifying exactly what he found so attractive about her. Though not a beauty queen like some of the nurses he had known, her looks struck a note that stirred his blood. He dozed off and dreamed of Clarissa smiling at him and her beautiful, moss green eyes.

Chapter Five
~ No Trespassing ~

Friday arrived for Clarissa's dinner date with Brent, and she anticipated an evening of learning more about him. This evening she wanted Brent to see her not as a savvy businesswoman, but as an attractive woman with romantic potential. In short, a hot babe, but an equal to a man, not a lamb for shearing or a plum for the picking. Since she met him at the Logan Antique Mall, she'd wondered if his interest in her could evolve into more than a business relationship.

Mindful of her duty to Ruthie, she fed her and let her out in the yard. As usual, the little pig went to the far corner, squatted, and then rooted for a minute in the grass near the porch. Clarissa raked the yard once a week and used grass clippings and Ruthie's waste in a compost pile. A clean and dainty animal, Ruthie seemed to approve of that.

"Okay, baby, come inside. Momma needs to get dressed." Ruthie climbed the steps and trotted into the house. Always attuned to Clarissa's moods, she rubbed up against her as she closed and locked the door.

In the bedroom, Clarissa went to her closet and pulled out a wraparound, *V*-necked, black and white dress she thought would please Brent. It emphasized all the right places. Paired with bright red heels and a coral necklace from her grandmother, it made her feel like a fashion model. A simple pair of coral earrings completed her ensemble. This dress would certainly catch Brent's attention. She swept her hair into a French roll and secured it with a black and white comb.

"Well, Ruthie, wish me luck. I'm off on my first date with a new man." She gave Ruthie a gentle pat on the head and the little pig snorted.

Clarissa picked up her purse and looked around for her car keys.

Ruthie came running with the keys in her little pink mouth. Laughing, Clarissa rubbed the pig's ears and retrieved her keys.

"You are such a sweet thing, aren't you, Ruthie." The little pig grunted in response.

Clarissa locked the door and headed to the car. The memory of Brent's fabulous smile accompanied her as she drove toward town, especially those sparkling blue eyes and his well-dressed hair. Her social skills were rusty, and she worried about appearing either too naïve or gauche.

After parking at the Logan Antique Mall, she got out of her car to look for Brent but didn't see him at first. Focusing on the mall, she located him sitting on a bench just in front of it. His blue blazer and black slacks emphasized his casual, but well-dressed appearance. When their eyes met, he flashed his dazzling smile and waved to her.

Clarissa didn't want to appear too anxious so she walked at a moderate pace to join him. The click of her unaccustomed high heels accompanied her as she crossed the asphalt parking lot. It made her wonder yet again how women could balance on those six-inchers.

As he surveyed her from head to toe, his smile reflected admiration, and his fabulous eyes glowed. "Haven't I seen you on the cover of *Glamour Magazine*?" His frank appreciation flattered her, but unused to compliments, she blushed.

He handed her a single red rose. "A beautiful rose for a lovely lady."

"Thank you." She breathed in its fragrance and smiled. Little things showed a man's character.

"No, thank you." The intensity of his gaze disconcerted and confused her as his eyes roved over her. "Shall we?" He held out his arm.

Caution made Clarissa hesitate. "Um, I'd rather we take our own cars, if you don't mind, just until we know each other better." She waited for his reaction, hoping he would understand and not be insulted.

"I see." A look of disappointment flitted across his face, but faded almost at once. He led her to her car and opened the driver's door for her. "Would you like to follow me to the restaurant?" He winked at her and she blushed again.

"Yes, fine." Relief washed over her that he hadn't taken offense.

After all, they had just met and only had coffee together. They really didn't know one another. Besides, what if he drove like a maniac? She looked over at his red Corvette and shuddered. Too many news stories showed the mangled wrecks of such racy cars.

Brent strolled over to his car and got in. He pulled out of the parking lot with Clarissa following close behind. It took about ten minutes to reach the restaurant. There, when she got out of her car, Brent reached for her hand.

He linked his arm with hers and led her toward the entrance of the Sandstone Restaurant. The façade reminded her of a renovated hotel. Inside, a sign read "Bistro Coming Soon." The hostess eyed Brent with interest.

"Hi, welcome to the Sandstone, my name's Sarah. Would you prefer a table by the window or bar?"

"I have a reservation under Soulder." Brent flashed a smile displaying his gleaming teeth.

As they followed the hostess through the restaurant, Clarissa guessed the décor was aimed at tourists. An old-fashioned wooden bar ran along one wall of the dining area, while murals of waterfalls and nature lined the other walls. One featured a large Shawnee Indian mural. Plants decorated the dining area. Clarissa hoped some imagination had also gone into the cuisine.

Tea light candles in simple holders resembling oil lamps graced each table. Similar looking lantern-style sconces graced the walls. The hostess led them to a leatherette booth for two near the back and lit the small candle on their table.

"Your server will be right with you." Sarah handed them each a menu and gave Brent a flirtatious smile as he took his.

He asked for a wine list, and the hostess provided one.

Brent glanced up with a raised eyebrow when Clarissa requested a glass of water. The hostess left them to explore their menus. It had a variety with chicken, fish, and steak.

"Do you like barbeque? The ribs here are excellent," Brent advised.

"Sometimes."

She smiled, remembering the last set of ribs she'd eaten at the Millstone. But not tonight—no way did she want the mess of eating ribs.

Anyway, most men liked steak.

"I love a good steak, too, every now and then."

"A woman after my own heart." Brent's grin looked as if he might eat her. "How about the flatiron steak?"

"What's that?" Clarissa looked puzzled. Because she seldom ate out, she had grown rusty on menu terms.

"It's a Cajun seasoned steak cooked in a flat, cast iron skillet, then they put another skillet on top to keep the steak flat," Brent explained.

"Sounds delicious." Her mouth watered.

The menu listed sautéed mushrooms, onions, and bell peppers served with the steak, a tossed salad, and a choice of mashed or baked potato. It all sounded like a good meal.

A young woman dressed in black approached. "Hi, my name's Trisha."

The server, Clarissa assumed. A black apron protected her dark skirt and blouse. Tall and slender, she wore her soft brown hair in a French braid.

"Have you decided what you'd like to order, or would you prefer a few more minutes?"

"We'll have flatiron steaks with all the fixings, please." Brent pointed to the menu and shot her one of his brilliant smiles.

"An excellent choice," the girl responded, her cheeks flushed pink. "How would you like your steaks?"

"Rare for me." Brent turned from her. "Clarissa?"

"Um, medium, please. I don't like it dripping blood."

Brent ginned at her. "Leave that to the men. We'll have the baked potatoes and Italian dressing on the salads, and a bottle of your best house wine." Brent handed Trisha the wine list.

"Um, is the house wine dry or sweet?" Clarissa said.

"We have both, miss."

Brent looked at Clarissa. "I think the lady prefers a sweeter wine, but I'd like the dry, so maybe we'd better have two glasses instead."

"I'll place your orders and be right back with the wine." Trisha winked at Brent and headed off to the kitchen.

Brent's good looks meant every woman found him attractive. Clarissa wondered if the server flirted with all the customers in hopes of a bigger tip. This was really their first date, and Brent did like attention. Still, would that make him less desirable husband material?

"So what have you been doing this week?" As he focused on her face, his gaze reflected intense interest.

She basked in the glow of his attention as his eyes sought her essence in an intimate way. How could he incite such feelings on such short acquaintance? Better to slow down. She took a deep breath and struggled to damp her racing pulse. He was a sexy man and sure to know how to please a woman, but she wanted more than a quick seduction. Time to cool it and change the subject.

"Not a lot, just keeping up with my billing business and savoring the nice weather."

Maybe if she stayed with chitchat, she could avoid focusing on the way Brent's clothes fit him and emphasized his trim physique. He must work out to stay so fit. She disliked the grunge look favored by trendy men these days, with uncombed hair and three-day beards.

She struggled to maintain a sensible conversation. "How about you?"

"The market keeps me busy just staying abreast of the best offerings. I'm working on some new stock deals for a couple of clients and making a few buys for myself."

"Tracking the stock market takes skill and guts," Clarissa observed.

"Yeah, it keeps me on my toes staying ahead of the losers these days." He gave her a crooked, knowing smile. "Stop by my office anytime you feel like it, and I'll see what I can do for you."

"I don't know..." She hesitated. Doing business with him wasn't quite what she had in mind. "I already have my investments pretty well set."

"I'm sure you do." He raised an eyebrow. "A businesswoman like you might want to consider some new investment opportunities. There are great bargains out there just now."

"Maybe later. I have your business card."

She'd had enough of investments and wanted to know more about him and especially about the women in his life. A man as well placed and with such fabulous looks had to have a past.

"Tell me more about yourself."

As if recognizing her unease, he leaned toward her with a flirtatious smile. "So, what kind of movies do you like? I prefer action adventures and comedies myself."

"I like lots of different kinds of movies, but mainly romance and comedies."

"No surprise there. Women always like romance, especially the tearjerkers. I'm glad you included comedies though. Maybe we could take in a movie sometime?" He quirked an eyebrow at her in an inviting manner.

"Sure, let me know when."

"How about the same time next Friday? We could eat dinner somewhere and then catch an early evening movie." He looked expectant.

That he wanted another date pleased her, but men liked women better when they had to work harder to gain their interest. "Why don't you call me Wednesday or Thursday, and we'll work out the details."

"You're on." He gave her a smile that could melt an iceberg, or thaw the heart of a lonely woman. He reached for her hand, but Trish the waitress returned with the wine.

"Here you go. Enjoy your wine. I'll be back with your orders as soon as they're ready." With a broad smile at Brent, she placed a basket with a fresh, hot loaf of bread, a small wooden cutting board with a serrated knife, and two small plates on the table.

"Oh, how wonderful, I love fresh baked bread." Clarissa beamed at him.

"With your sparkling eyes, you remind me of a wide-eyed child at Christmas. Here, I'll cut you a slice." Brent handed her one of the small plates with a nice sized slice of bread.

"Thank you." She accepted the plate from him, and their fingers brushed. His touch sent warmth flowing through her veins.

* * * *

Friday night, David Claremont arrived in town to join a crowd of about fifty people. Everyone was drinking, talking, and visiting local vendor tables set up along the street. The people examined the wares and sampled hors d'oeuvres.

"David!" Donna Gilead, the real estate lady, came to his side with a big grin on her face. Her tight-fitting blue dress revealed a bit more than he wanted to see.

"I'm so glad you could make it. How've you been? Are you settling in all right?"

"Yes," David responded.

He glanced around the crowd looking to see if Clarissa was there. He wanted to know more about her, especially since he found out she was the biller for his medical practice. Guilt for being so rude the first day they met still plagued his conscience.

"You simply must allow me to introduce you to some of our more prominent members of the community." Like a boa constrictor, Donna linked her arm with his and steered him toward the table with the most food.

Reluctantly, he let her lead him. He suspected that if he hadn't been a doctor and paid cash for his cabin, she might show less interest in him. Money and status preoccupied her.

She approached a plump, grayish-blond-haired woman by the food table. "Judy, this is Dr. David Claremont. He's the new doctor in Dr. Jennings' office. He'll eventually take over the practice when Dr. Jennings retires."

Donna turned to David. "Dr. Claremont, Ms. Judy Finnegan, she run's the Café Corner restaurant here in town and makes the best blueberry pie you'll ever eat." She picked up a little plastic cup with a spoon-sized piece of blueberry pie in it just big enough for a sample.

David smiled pleasantly at Miss Finnegan and shook her hand. "Nice to meet you, Ms. Finnegan."

"Likewise, Dr. Claremont; this town is fortunate to have you."

David followed Donna's lead by selecting a sample of the famous blueberry pie. One bite made him want more. Mmmm, it was delicious. Mrs. Gilead was right—he never tasted anything so good.

"This is the best blueberry pie I've ever eaten," he said to Judy Finnegan.

"Thank you, Dr. Claremont." She acknowledged his praise with a knowing smile.

"Please, call me David."

"Well, we're off," Donna said. "I want David to meet the mayor. Have you seen him tonight?"

"Yes, he's over there speaking with Mr. Elkins." Judy pointed to a short, fat, balding man a few tables down. He looked to be in his early forties with a button-down shirt and tie framed by a pinstripe brown suit. David nodded a good-bye to Judy as Donna steered him toward the mayor.

"Mayor Maynard, I'd like you to meet Dr. David Claremont. He's working with Dr. Jennings. He moved here about a week ago, and we're so lucky to have him," Donna gushed to the mayor.

"David, this is Marshall Maynard, our town's mayor. If it weren't for him, we'd all be in trouble." She smiled at the mayor as if she shared an intimate acquaintance.

"Very nice to meet you." David shook hands and applauded the mayor's firm grip. He hated weak handshakes or sweaty palms.

"Likewise," the mayor answered. "You're a lucky man to be working with Dr. Jennings. He's been taking good care of our people ever since I was a boy."

"Yes, I'm sure I'll learn a lot from his experiences and his wisdom."

Donna dragged David away to mingle with the other townsfolk and to visit the various vendor tables representing the local shop owners in town. To his disappointment, he never once saw Clarissa. They would be working together like it or not, and they were next-door neighbors. He wanted things to be civilized between them and maybe just a bit warmer than that. He'd seen a lot of children and teenagers, but few women his age who weren't accompanied by a man.

* * * *

After dinner, Brent suggested they stop at the local dance spot down the street. The place was a bar with a pocket dance floor and a disc jockey. Brent secured a table next to the dance floor. The music varied from soft rock to swing, and even a waltz or two.

"So, what would you like to drink?" Brent looked toward the bar.

"Um, after wine with dinner, maybe just a Sprite," Clarissa responded.

He soon returned with a beer for himself and the Sprite for her. The

DJ had just begun a waltz.

"Come," Brent said, taking her hand and leading her onto the dance floor.

He drew her close and whirled her into the dance. Clarissa soon lost herself in the flow of the music as Brent led them around the other dancers with never a misstep. Every time Brent spun her around and then pulled her into his arms, her heart raced and her face flushed. No one dared cut in the way Brent held onto her.

He drew her close in slow numbers and left her breathless in the swing dances. In his arms, she savored the scent of his spicy aftershave and the security and warmth of his embrace. Emotion held sway, and she wanted to be held like this forever and never let go.

They attracted admiring glances on the dance floor. One or two people made comments about couples in love. Others applauded as they left the dance floor.

By the time the DJ played "Goodnight, Irene," she could hardly stand on her own two feet. Once the music stopped, her aching feet protested. Those heels looked nice, but her feet weren't used to them.

"Happy?" Brent asked.

"You're a great dancer," Clarissa observed. She had learned to dance before she moved to the country two years ago for fun and exercise, but hadn't had an occasion to dance much since.

"So are you," he replied slipping his arm around her waist. "It's rare for a woman to keep up with me on the dance floor." Pride colored his words.

Warmth flowed through Clarissa's veins. Could it be the wine, or did Brent cause these strange but pleasant sensations? He overwhelmed her senses and made her long for more.

He opened the car door for her and helped her into the seat. Leaning closer, his mouth approached hers. A tingling sensation invaded her as his tongue explored her mouth. The kiss seemed to last forever and enthralled her. Too soon, Clarissa had to break off the kiss for air.

Pulling back, she smiled up at him, blushing. "I...I had a great time."

He responded with his dazzling smile. "I'll call you sometime next week to set up a time for our movie date,"

"Sounds great. I'll be looking forward to it. Thanks for dinner, dancing, the beautiful rose, and..." She almost said *and that amazing kiss*. "I really enjoyed the evening."

"You're more than welcome. You're an interesting woman and I...find you tantalizing." He left her with her thoughts as he walked to his car.

* * * *

When Clarissa arrived home, a peculiar sight met her. A small, skinny, tricolored basset pup huddled in front of the door looked up at her as she stepped onto the porch. She reached down and petted the puppy.

"What an adorable little thing you are. Where did you come from?"

The little puppy whined. Clarissa wondered how the dog had ended on her front porch. She really didn't want or need a dog, yet here the puppy sat, tail wagging. The bright brown eyes looked full of hope.

"What am I to do with you? Has someone lost you?" She leaned down and scratched the soft ears. The puppy rolled on its back, all four feet in the air. "So you're a little girl."

Clarissa sighed. "After those vicious dogs prowling around the other night, I can't leave you out here. I'll try to find you a home. In the meantime, you'll have to stay with me." She opened the door, and the puppy followed her inside.

Ruthie trotted up to Clarissa to have the soft spot behind her ears rubbed. "I've brought you a friend, Ruthie."

The puppy nosed Ruthie. The little pig jumped back, stared at the pup, and then looked at Clarissa. The puppy rolled over on her back again.

"It's all right, baby. She just wants to be friends."

Ruthie sniffed the squirming puppy and snorted. This time the puppy rolled to her feet and tripped over her trailing ears as she scuttled back. Laughing, Clarissa patted them both. Ruthie sat on her haunches and watched the long-eared pup. The puppy eyed Ruthie and whimpered.

"Just tolerate one another, okay?"

She kicked off her shoes and pulled off her dress, grabbing her robe from the bedroom. Then she led both animals to the kitchen and gave

Ruthie some grapes. Next, she put a few pieces of leftover meat in a dish for the pup that vanished in two gulps.

"Guess I'll have to get some puppy food for you."

After settling Ruthie in her basket and the puppy in a box with an old blanket for the night, Clarissa lay in bed thinking about her first date with Brent. The puppy whined, and she reached down to pet it.

"It's okay, baby, you're safe with me." The puppy seemed soothed and closed her eyes. She snuggled close to Ruthie's basket.

Clarissa wondered if Brent thought about her and anticipated their second date. Despite not liking some of his questions, his male attractiveness stirred her senses, and she looked forward to the movie with him. The small town of Logan offered few eligible professional men.

Tony had left her so emotionally bruised and suspicious, she no longer knew how to react or even how to judge a man's intentions. She had no idea how Brent felt about her. She fell asleep thinking of Brent and that kiss, but ended up dreaming about David Claremont. In her dream, Brent turned into David holding her close. His breath on her neck made her whole body burn with an intense fire.

* * * *

The next day, she placed an ad in the local newspaper to find the pup a home. If no one claimed the animal, she would resign herself to becoming the new owner. After their initial meeting, Ruthie didn't appear to mind the small puppy.

"What shall I call you?" Clarissa put a finger to her lip as she pondered the thought. "I know," she said after a few minutes. "I'll call you Penny. How does that sound?"

Penny was the name of one of her neighbor's dogs when she lived in Columbus. The dog had been a beagle and looked kind of like this puppy, but with shorter ears. She looked to Penny and then to Ruthie. Then, after a few more minutes, she nodded.

"Penny it is."

* * * *

Jimmy arrived at David's front door Saturday at six o'clock sharp. He prided himself on being on time and following through with promises.

His knock echoed on the cabin door.

He hoped the doc remembered their hunting trip. He remained as enthusiastic about their morning plans as he had been that day at the doctor's office. The door opened on a grinning David.

"Hello, come on in. I'm just finishing breakfast." David led Jimmy through the front hallway lined with wooden pegs for hanging coats. Jimmy followed him to a spacious kitchen with oak cabinets and a solid oak table with four chairs in the center of the room. A few boxes lay around, as the doctor hadn't quite finished settling into his new home.

Jimmy admired the beauty of this roomy log cabin. The newly refinished oak cabinets and oak furniture made the place look different from when Old Man Jenkin owned it. It appeared much cleaner and brighter now that it had a new owner. He almost wished his house had this same rustic style. He'd added on to the farmhouse to accommodate his growing family.

"Have a cup of coffee." David handed Jimmy a mug. "Cream and sugar are on the table, and I've some eggs on the stove."

"Thanks, I already ate, but I'll take the coffee." Jimmy smiled. David appeared in a good mood today. He acted so much friendlier than their first encounter when he had tried to give David a newspaper.

The doc filled Jimmy's mug with fresh hot coffee and the two of them sat down at the kitchen table to discuss their plans.

"I have my 12-gage all cleaned and ready to go." David beamed with pride.

"I have the old Smith and Wesson my dad handed down to me from his dad. I hope we bag us a couple of nice turkeys." Jimmy grinned from ear to ear. "Just think, come deer season, we can get us a deer or two."

After their coffee, the two of them headed out the door and set off to walk down the road toward the Wilford place. As they passed Ms. Wilford's mailbox, a woman yelled at them in an annoyed voice.

"No hunting on my land." She pointed to a No Trespassing sign anchored in the ground by her mailbox. They turned and looked as Clarissa approached them with a menacing stride, followed by Ruthie and a small basset hound trotting behind her. She glowered at them. Jimmy hoped she'd settle down and not yell at the doc.

Chapter Six
~ Lunch Date ~

At the mailbox, Clarissa glared at Jimmy Johnson and David Claremont toting guns as she stood by the No Trespassing sign. Ruthie and Penny hovered at her heels. Hot anger engulfed her.

"I told you before, Jimmy Johnson, how I feel about hunting and trapping on my land." She stood with her hands on her hips and confronted the hunters.

"We wasn't gonna hunt on your land, ma'am. Honest. We're off to Old Man Rodger's place just down the road. He told me I could hunt on his land anytime, and we're hoping to nab us a couple of turkeys for dinner." Jimmy's explanation did nothing to soothe her, and even Penny stared at the two with watchful eyes.

"Why don't you buy a turkey at the grocery store like other people do?"

"No sport in that. Besides, we help control the turkey population, else they'd eat everything in sight," Jimmy said.

"Humph, you can't hunt on my land. I won't have grown men killing living creatures for pleasure. If I had my way, they'd outlaw such things."

She turned and started to stalk off, her chin in the air, but tripped and almost fell when Penny danced between her feet. A strong pair of arms grabbed and steadied her. She blinked and looked up to see David Claremont's hands holding her. A vision of her dream from the night before came to mind. She backed away, this time watching out for the dog.

"Who's the new pup?" Jimmy looked at Penny. "She's awful cute."

41

Clarissa stared down at the pup and smiled. "I don't know where she came from. She was on my porch when I came home the other night, so I put an ad in the paper to find her a home. Meanwhile, I call her Penny." She reached down and rubbed behind Penny's long droopy ears.

"I've a basset hound myself. They're loyal and good hunting dogs. She might grow on ya after a bit." He smiled down at Penny.

"No way," Clarissa sputtered. "Not this one, no hunting for her. If I can't find her a home, I'll adopt her. At least that way I can save one creature's life." She spun on her heels and marched toward the house, this time careful to ensure Penny stayed away from her feet.

"Ms. Wilford," David Claremont called after her. "You forgot your mail." He held out a handful of envelopes and advertisements.

"Thank you, Dr. Claremont." Flustered, Clarissa reached for her mail.

"I didn't see you at the town festival last night," he said.

"Oh, I…um…was busy," she stammered, not sure what to say. No way would she mention her date with Brent. She owed this man no explanation. "I'm not much for that sort of thing."

"Too bad. I'd hoped we might have a chance to chat. We got off to a bit of a rough start the first time we met." He smiled in apology.

"Oh?" She raised an eyebrow. At least he realized he needed one. "I stop by your office Mondays. Perhaps we can talk then." She had too much work to do to spend time on idle chitchat.

"Monday it is then." He nodded in agreement.

Clarissa turned back toward her house with Ruthie and Penny, the new puppy. Penny was tripping on her long droopy ears and tumbling head over paws. Laughter floated back from the two men as they walked away. Her cheeks burned.

What a perfect match she and the puppy made, each tripping over themselves when they tried to walk. Question was who was clumsier, her or the pup? As for that new neighbor of hers, she didn't quite know what to think of David Claremont. On one hand, he irritated her with an arrogant manner so typical of young doctors, but on the other hand, he had manners, his flannel shirt emphasized his broad shoulders, and his jeans encased sturdy legs and lean hips. If only she could make up her mind as to whether or not she liked him.

* * * *

Jimmy and David continued down the road toward the Rodgers' land.

"I'm sorry about that," Jimmy said to David. "I should've warned you how she feels about hunting."

"No worries. I know now never to let her see me with a gun in my hand on her land." Smiling, David patted Jimmy on the back. "What do ya say we forget her and focus on the turkeys instead? I hear they're a wily lot and not easy to hunt."

"Yeah, they sure are," Jimmy said.

The doc seemed like a real nice fellow after all. He must have just caught him at a bad time the day they first met. At least he hadn't been so keen that day when he tried to offer him that free newspaper. Jimmy knew from experience that first impressions weren't always accurate.

"I'm looking forward to deer season and hope to shoot a couple of 'em. We'll need that meat to get through the winter. With everything so pricey these days, it's a good thing I always bag my limit." He liked havin' the doc as a hunting buddy. It had reassured Ellen when he told her about the doc goin' with him.

The morning flew past. Tracking turkeys took skill, but Jimmy knew where to look. Before David knew it, they each shot a turkey and tagged them.

"Not bad for our first hunting trip together." Jimmy beamed from ear to ear.

"Yeah, we have some plump birds. Now we need someone to pluck and clean them?"

"Me and Ellen, my wife, can. I know all about cleaning 'em, and she's the best cook when it comes to fixing them for dinner. You just come with me and you'll see."

They saw no sign of Miz Wilford when they passed her place on their return. At the doc's, they piled into the old Buick, and checked the turkeys with the nearest hunters' station. Then, Jimmy drove home.

Ellen greeted them as they entered the house. "How did your hunting go? Must have been good." She smiled as she watched her husband hold up his kill.

"Honey, this is David Claremont, the new doctor in town. He just moved into the old Jenkin place next to Miz Wilford. Doc, this is my wife Ellen, and she'll cook a feast you'll never forget." Jimmy smiled at his wife.

"Nice to meet you, Dr. Claremont, and welcome to our home." Ellen shook hands with the doc.

Jimmy hugged her, proud of his beautiful wife. Her blond hair still shone and her blue eyes twinkled. At only five and a half feet, she just reached Jimmy's shoulder.

"Thank you, it's nice to meet you, ma'am. Jimmy didn't tell me how pretty you were." The doc smiled and looked around at the place.

Jimmy wished it looked less run-down, but he still considered the old farmhouse beautiful. Ellen had decorated the large front living room with blue and white striped wallpaper and a blue ceiling. She even found some dark blue couches and chairs and a dark wooden coffee table at a thrift store and cleaned them until they looked good as new.

"You have a lovely home, Ms. Johnson," Doc said.

Ellen blushed. "Thank you, Dr. Claremont—just call me Ellen."

"I will if you call me David."

"Kids, come meet the new doctor," Jimmy hollered up the stairs. His three children came racing down—two boys and blonde Julie, the spitting image of her mother. Booker trotted at Julie's heels.

"Hey, mister, I remember you," Jimmy Junior said.

"I remember you, too, sport. How's the tummy?" Doc asked.

"I'm Julie, and this is my dog Booker," the blonde girl said. "Will you make me better if I get sick?"

"Of course I will, Julie. It would be my pleasure." The doc smiled at her.

"This is my oldest son, Tommy." Jimmy motioned to the boy standing tall and proud next to his mother, brother, and sister.

"Nice to meet you, Tommy," Doc said. "You must be proud of your dad. He's a fine hunter."

"Yeah, he's been teaching me how to hunt and skin deer." Tommy's pride shone on his face and echoed in his voice.

"We raise our vegetables and fruits," Jimmy said with pride. "The frost came early in the spring last year, so we lost most of the pears. Ellen keeps a dozen chickens and two roosters, so we have all the eggs we need. I also have a small greenhouse I use in the winter. If you need fresh vegetables or eggs, just let me know."

"I've never had much luck with a garden. No time really." The doc sighed.

"You're a doctor. You don't need to grub in the dirt. Sometimes I wish for book smarts or an education. At least I have country smarts, and we eat well."

Booker, Julie's basset hound, sniffed at the doc's boots.

"Hi ya, Booker old boy," the doc said and scratched the dog's ears.

Old Booker loved that and rolled over on his back with all four legs in the air. "Looks like you made a friend, Doc. Like Ms. Wilford's pup, he just showed up here one day with no collar, and Julie adopted him. Have to get these turkeys cleaned. Why don't you have a beer on the porch while I do it?"

"Sure, but don't hesitate to ask for help if you need it."

"The porch is this way." Ellen led David to a small side porch with two rocking chairs and a wooden bench. "Jimmy and I met in grade school when we were ten. He used to tease me by pulling my braids. We got married after high school, then Jimmy's parents died and left him the house. A year after that, Tommy came along."

"High-school sweethearts, you two have quite a history together." David smiled at them.

"Yes, we do, and I wouldn't trade him for anything." Ellen smiled back. "I'll be back in a minute with your beer and a plate of fresh baked cookies." She headed into the house leaving David to admire the rolling tree-covered hills from the broad porch.

He thought about Clarissa and her little pig and now the new little pup. He found it interesting that she had chosen a pig for a pet over a cat or a dog. He never would have thought of anyone having a pet pig. He wondered if Clarissa would ever be a friend. She was nice- looking, had brains, and had caught his interest.

"Here you go." Ellen returned and handed him a bottle of beer and a small plate of cookies. "I baked these fresh this morning. I hope you enjoy them."

"I'm sure I will." David took the plate and the beer from her. "So, what do you do around here for fun when you're not hunting, gardening, or looking after kids?"

"Well, we often go camping across the way at Lake Logan and do some fishing and swimming as well. The kids love it out here, and Jimmy and I grew up in the country. I lived with my parents just down the road before Jimmy and I got married and we moved in here."

"It's a beautiful area. Looks like lots of good hunting."

"You've got that right." She sat in one of the rocking chairs with a cookie and a glass of lemonade.

"Mommy, mommy." Little Jimmy appeared. "Can I take the doc and show him our garden?"

"May I," Ellen corrected him, "and yes, you may."

Jimmy Junior led David by the hand through the house and out into the big backyard. To the right of the yard, he saw a large cultivated garden with neat rows of vegetables and tomato plants tied to stakes in the ground. Wooden frames with clear plastic covered the garden during early spring and late fall.

"We got tomatoes, potatoes, green beans, cabbage, corn, eggplant, squash, peas, green peppers, onions, just about every vegetable you can think of," Jimmy Junior rattled off.

"That's great. Bet it keeps you busy weeding and picking the ripe ones." David appreciated the hard work and patience Jimmy, Ellen, and the kids must put into the garden.

"Yeah, but Pa and you get to go deer huntin' and fishin'.'"

"Here you go, Doc." Jimmy handed him a plastic bag with a cleaned turkey. "It's all ready to go. All ya have to do is cook it."

"That was quick," David said as he took the bag from Jimmy. "Your son here was showing me your garden. Nice, but a lot of work."

"Yeah, we work on it almost every day." Jimmy took his son's hand and started toward the house. "Got to get this turkey to my wife, so she can fix it for supper tonight. Would you join us?"

"No, but thanks anyway. I have to get home and do some more unpacking before tomorrow so I can spend at least part of my Sunday relaxing." David followed Jimmy through the house and out the front door. "I'll take a rain check on that turkey dinner."

"Sure thing," Jimmy said. "I'll let you know the next time we have turkey."

David turned to Ellen. "It was nice to meet you, Ellen"

"Nice to meet you, too, David. Be sure to join us for dinner sometime soon, okay?"

"My pleasure. You two are lucky to have such a nice home and beautiful children."

"Thank you, take care." She waved as Jimmy led them back to the old beat-up Buick, and the two of them drove off toward David's home.

"So, would you like to go fishing with me next Saturday?" Jimmy said.

"Yeah, sure, that sounds like fun."

Jimmy stopped in the driveway and let him out. "I'll call you, and we can set a time." Driving away, Jimmy waved as he left David standing in his driveway waving back.

David entered the house to find Jasper waiting for him. "Hey Jazz, how are ya, buddy? Did you miss me?" Jasper responded by meowing and weaving himself between David's legs.

He headed for his kitchen to put away his turkey and get Jasper some fresh food and water. He stroked the cat and thought about the pleasant day. Who would have thought after living in the city for so long that he would adapt to country living so easily?

* * * *

Monday morning, as Clarissa drove toward Dr. Jennings' office, she thought about her second date with Brent, now only a few days away. His smooth dancing and expert kissing left her longing for more. She hoped he found her as attractive as she found him, and wondered if he could be the one. A future with someone like him promised everything she'd ever wanted. Thoughts of Brent and his come-hither smile kept her humming as she drove.

She intended to drop off her finished work and pick up the latest records on new patient visits.

As she entered the office, Geneva smiled at her. "Good morning, Clarissa."

"Good morning." Her good mood continued and she smiled back. "Such a beautiful day. I've finished last week's work and stopped to pick up the files for the recent office visits." She handed the completed folders to Geneva and took the waiting stack from their customary place on the corner of the desk. "How's the new doctor?"

"I like him, and he's good with the patients." Geneva raved about David Claremont's abilities, looks, and personality. "Everyone loves him, and he takes a load off of Dr. Jennings."

Remembering her promise on Saturday to talk with the young doctor for a few minutes, Clarissa nodded. "Great, is he here now?"

Despite having gotten off on the wrong foot with Dr. Claremont, it made good business sense to get on well with her clients. His rudeness on their first meeting and his hunting with Jimmy Johnson had only increased her negative view of him.

"Sure, I'll see if he's free." Geneva went toward the back of the office and knocked on a closed door. "Dr. Claremont, our biller Ms. Wilford is here to see you."

"I'll be right there," a pleasant tenor voice called from behind the door.

"Have a seat if you'd like. He'll be out in a minute."

"Thanks, that's fine." Clarissa stumbled to the nearest seat in the waiting room and grabbed a magazine to browse through while she waited on David. Maybe she could find an article on how to be graceful instead of clumsy.

It had been almost a year since she had sat in the waiting area of a doctor's office. She always hated waiting, and for some reason doctors took forever. It made her wonder about their sense of time and their priorities.

To her surprise, a minute later, David appeared and held out his hand in greeting. "Glad to see you this morning. I hoped you'd stop by."

"I always do at the beginning of each week to return the completed records and get those waiting for processing."

His firm, warm handshake sent shivers down her spine. Whoa, just a handshake, nothing more. Besides, she only wanted to maintain good client relations.

"Why not join me for lunch today? I'd like the company, and it would give me a chance to apologize to you for my rudeness the first day we met. I realize now you were just being neighborly." He flashed a big, bright smile at her that could melt the biggest iceberg.

"Uh, sure. What time and where shall I meet you?"

"Say eleven forty-five at the Café Corner restaurant. Ms. Finnegan makes the best blueberry pie, and I have it on good authority her home cooking is the best in all of Logan."

"I have a few errands to do so I'll meet you there. I'm sure you're in for a busy morning with your patients."

Clarissa left him smiling at her and waved a quick good-bye. She still harbored mixed feelings toward him, but at least he appeared pleasant and determined to reassure her.

* * * *

Entering the homey Café Corner promptly at eleven forty-five, Clarissa eyed the blue checked curtains. They added to the pleasant country atmosphere, and the aroma from kitchen promised good things to eat. She saw David already seated at a corner booth, studying a menu.

She sat down opposite him. "Have you been waiting long?"

"Actually, no I just got here a minute ago myself." He grinned at her.

"So, what looks good today?" Clarissa scanned the typed menu, glad to have a focus beyond the doctor's rugged good looks.

"I'm told the food is excellent, and I can personally attest to the mouth-watering blueberry pie." His broad smile sent those little shivers down her spine. She fought to keep her face from turning red.

Get a grip, girl. How could she consider this man attractive? She hated hunters. Besides, he'd bought the old Jenkin place and hunted with Jimmy Johnson. They probably guzzled beer and left their cans around to litter the roadside. Brent didn't hunt, thank heaven. Clarissa struggled to focus on the menu choices.

"Miss, can I get you something to drink?" A young attractive blonde stood in front of Clarissa with her pen and pad, ready to take her drink order.

"Um, I'll have a glass of your raspberry iced tea." Clarissa smiled, satisfied with her choice. "You have any specials today?"

"We have teriyaki grilled salmon with wild rice and broccoli, and our featured soup today is potato cheese soup."

Surprised not to hear meatloaf or country fried steak, Clarissa's mouth watered. "Yum, sounds wonderful." She could taste the salty, sweet salmon already. "I'll have the soup and the special."

"For you, sir?" The server looked at David. Clarissa thought for a moment her eyes might pop out of her head. The doctor clearly impressed the girl, but David didn't act as though he harbored any sort of attraction toward the girl, which pleased Clarissa.

"I'll have the same," he said without hesitation. "I know a good choice when I hear it."

The server left to place their orders and get Clarissa's tea.

"So how is everything going for you with Doctor Jennings?"

"Great, he's a wonderful doctor and has genuine rapport with his patients. The townspeople I've met have accepted me like one of their own." He beamed with pleasure. "How about you? How's life treating you?" He studied her face with sincere interest.

The intensity of his gaze disconcerted her. "I'm pretty busy with the billing and pricing my latest pieces for my antique glassware business."

"Really?" He looked intrigued. "How long have you been selling antique glassware? My mother might be interested in some of your pieces. She's collected the stuff since I was little."

"I've sold pieces for about two years now. After I found my first piece at the Logan Antique Mall, I fell in love with beautiful, unique glassware, especially pieces made in and around Ohio. I had no idea this area supported so many glassmakers. I started buying and selling pieces online and then rented my own little space in the mall." Her excitement and passion colored her voice.

The server set her raspberry iced tea in front of her.

"Thank you," Clarissa said.

The doctor gazed at her with intense green eyes. They reminded her of shadowed forest glades. A rollercoaster took over her stomach.

Chapter Seven
~ Romance ~

"So you sell collectable glassware," David said as they continued to talk over lunch at the Café Corner. "I'd love to do something like that, but my work keeps me busy. When I have a little free time, I ride my Honda cycle. Then there's hunting, fishing, and sometimes serenading Jasper with my violin as he meows along," The merry twinkle in his eyes mesmerized Clarissa.

"The violin? You play the violin?" That took talent.

"At least Jazz doesn't howl. I play mostly classical pieces like Bach and Mozart. I even play a little Bluegrass sometimes. He likes that, too, but prefers the classics."

"I'm impressed. I never mastered an instrument. I tried once, but I hated practicing." She grimaced.

"Sometimes I would cut my practice short, but Mom always reminded me."

Uncertain she wanted to talk about families, she tried to focus on what else he'd said. "I've never ridden a motorcycle. Guess it saves on gas."

"Yeah. I've had it for about ten years. My dad helped me rebuild it when I was younger so I know all about keeping it running. I don't ride it that often but I really love to feel the wind when I do. I could take you riding on it sometime if you'd like."

"Sounds great," Clarissa blushed and reached for her tea.

The glass, wet from condensation, slipped from her fingers and spilled. Luckily, she hadn't left much. Nonetheless, the red liquid formed a small pool. The server rushed over and wiped up the spill.

"Can I get you another?"

"No, I'd just spill it, but thanks anyway." She turned to David, anxious to cover her clumsiness. "I used to go fishing with my dad when I was younger, and I kind of miss it."

"Sounds great, we could fish and do a picnic lunch." David grinned like a kid.

Clarissa smiled her warmest smile at him, pleased to hear he liked something besides hunting. This side of him surprised and pleased her.

"Sometimes there just doesn't seem to be enough hours in the day. Billing keeps me busy much of the time. That's why I love weekends. Time to kick back and relax."

"Same here, but I want to see more of Logan and get to know my new neighbors." His interested smile unnerved her a little.

She found David much too attractive for her peace of mind, but his guns and their business relationship put him off limits. At least Brent had no such obstacles. A handsome and savvy businessman, he knew how to dance and push all the right buttons. Best of all, he didn't hunt. He had everything she wanted and maybe more.

So, why did she feel the need to justify her feelings for Brent every time she was with David? She'd have to be blind not to find David attractive—who wouldn't? But she had to avoid that if she wanted Brent. She should only focus on eligible men, and that meant Brent.

The server arrived with their cheesy potato soup, and the two started eating.

"Mmmm, this is great." Clarissa savored every spoonful, and David looked like he enjoyed his soup as much as she did.

"I have it from an authority that the food here is excellent, and I have to agree." He took another spoonful of the creamy hot soup.

About the time they finished, the server whisked away the empty bowls and set their teriyaki-grilled salmon before them. Clarissa marveled at the succulent salmon, perfect wild rice, and steamed broccoli, all in all a superb meal. She had no idea this local restaurant produced such great food. Even the presentation of the dish with a thin slice of lemon, a sprig of fresh parsley, and a few mint leaves appealed.

"I'll have to come here more often," she said.

A plump, grey-haired woman approached their table. "Dr.

Claremont, how nice to see you."

David rose to greet her. "Ms. Finnegan, I'd like you to meet Clarissa Wilford."

"Hello, Clarissa. It's nice to see you've finally made it."

"I'm only sorry it's taken me so long. The food here is great. I really loved the salmon."

"Thank you, most people like it. I trust you enjoyed your meal, Doctor." She smiled at David and nodded to Clarissa before moving to the next table.

"She makes the best blueberry pie. I've never had any better than they serve here."

"I'm really full, and I don't often eat dessert."

"You have to try it. We could share a piece."

Clarissa hesitated as she pondered whether to indulge. She had enjoyed the food so far, and she loved a good dessert.

"At the town festival Friday night, Ms. Finnegan provided samples of her blueberry pie at her booth. It's a perfect ending to a great meal."

David's enthusiasm swayed her along with her own temptation. "Okay, if you promise to eat most of it."

"Sure, an excellent idea, I couldn't manage a whole piece myself anyway."

The server cleared away their dishes and brought them a large piece of the blueberry pie topped with real whipped cream and two forks. Within a few minutes, the pie disappeared. Replete, Clarissa leaned back in her chair.

"You were right about that pie. Too many lunches here, and I'll gain weight."

When the server brought the check, Clarissa and David both reached for it at the same time. Their hands touched, and David grabbed hers, holding it in his for just a moment.

"My treat," he said. "You can get the tip instead, and next time we each pay, okay? I'd feel better if you let me pay today as a peace offering after our rocky start."

"I guess I could accept that, but only if you promise we each pay next time." Clarissa agreed, anxious for him to release her hand.

He made her giddy, and she wanted to fill the silences. Anything to avoid too much intimacy.

She beamed at him to let him know she had forgiven his former rudeness. As for his hunting, she couldn't accept it, but it had nothing to do with their working relationship. Yet it didn't seem to matter what her mind was telling her when her body refused to cooperate.

"It's a deal." He grinned at her, releasing her hand, and passed the bill and his Visa card to the server.

The girl smiled at both of them as if she considered them a pair of lovers instead of co-workers. David held the door for Clarissa as they left the restaurant.

* * * *

Arriving home from the wonderful lunch, Clarissa remembered her conversation with David and his easy manners. He had insisted on walking her to her car. His manners reassured her he wasn't the rude, obnoxious man she originally considered him. At least they could work together without animosity as long as she kept things professional.

A howl sounded in the woods. Darn wild dogs. She hoped they stayed away from Ruthie and Penny. Neither of them could defend themselves against feral dogs.

Clarissa's pets welcomed her, tails wagging, as she opened the front door.

"Ruthie, Penny, I missed you both."

She stooped down and scooped up Ruthie to cuddle her. Then, she set Ruthie down to pet Penny and rub her round tummy.

"How are you, Penny? Let's go for a short walk, shall we?" Grabbing Ruthie's harness, leash, and an old leash of Ruthie's for Penny, she headed for the front door. The three of them set off down the road toward David's place.

"What do you think guys, Brent or David? David is nice, but he's my client. Brent has loads of charm and is so romantic. Besides, David kills deer."

Penny and Ruthie just looked up at her as if they hadn't a clue and only wanted to walk. The memory of David with her pets surfaced. Would Ruthie and Penny get along as well with Brent? Well, she'd find out soon enough, and then she'd know what kind of a future they might have.

She wondered what Brent was doing. Was he selling investments to one of his clients? Maybe he was thinking about her, too. At that, her ears started buzzing.

* * * *

When she returned from the walk, the answering machine blinked off and on again. She played it, happy to hear a message from Brent. His voice came through loud and clear.

"Hey, beautiful, I just called to ask you to meet me outside the movie theater in Logan at five on Friday evening. If you can't make it, call me back and let me know, otherwise I'll meet you there."

Well, he must be interested since he hadn't wasted any time calling to confirm their Friday date. The other messages came from telemarketers who hung up when no one answered. One number showed up on her caller ID as Trade Industries. Trade Industries? Strange, she'd never heard of them before.

The last message came from her brother Cliff. "Hey, Sis, please join me for dinner at six Saturday evening at our favorite Japanese restaurant, Shogun Steakhouse, for sushi. Love ya, later."

She really didn't like driving to Columbus, but she hadn't seen Cliff for a while. *"I'll see you at the Shogun Saturday at 6,"* she replied to Cliff in a quick e-mail. She remembered the last time they'd eaten there and how much she loved the Japanese décor and music. Cliff had invited her to celebrate his recent real estate acquisition of a small apartment complex. She kept trying to talk him into moving to the country, but he had always been a city boy and wouldn't leave the city.

She'd been a city girl too, but she had discovered the inspiring serenity of country life and loved it. After one glorious week at her Aunt Mary's farm in Sugar Grove, Ohio, she fell in love with the beautiful farms and forested hills. Not long after that, Clarissa traded her city home for a country one, a move she never regretted.

Sighing, she spent the rest of the afternoon working on her new billing accounts and finishing old ones. She even managed to select and price a few of her newest glassware pieces to add to her booth on her next visit to the Mall. At least once a week, she stopped there to check on things and spruce up her display. It paid to provide something new for her regular buyers and to check the suggestion box for customer requests.

After dinner, she and her pets relaxed on the back porch while she worked on her painting of Ruthie. She painted landscapes mostly, but this was her first one of an animal. She used a photo she had taken of Ruthie so she didn't have to contend with the little pig moving while she painted, but could still refer to the live animal as needed.

Ruthie explored the backyard, looking for more acorns while Penny dug up a bone Clarissa had given her, which the pup had buried earlier. Clarissa thanked the squirrel for cleaning up the acorns. Ruthie didn't need those.

Jasper, David's cat, paraded along the fence line as if to say *"Ha ha, you can't get me."* Ruthie stared and snorted at Jasper while Penny sniffed and barked. The cat leaped to the ground next to Ruthie, and to Clarissa's surprise, began to purr. He tried to rub up against Ruthie in a friendly manner. She sniffed at him, but didn't squeal or run. It made Clarissa want to laugh. Penny didn't frighten him at all, and Jasper even licked at her droopy ears.

* * * *

The week flew by. Clarissa focused on her billing practice, priced a couple of new glassware pieces for her showcase, and worked on Ruthie's portrait. She even managed to look up Trade Industries on the Internet, and discovered they were a big investment firm specializing in properties to develop. How strange. They must have called her by mistake. What could they possibly want with her? Maybe Brent had given them her name. She'd ask him tonight. The night of their next date had come, and she wanted to look her best.

Wasting no time, Clarissa proceeded to dress. She chose a dark blue dress with shiny silver buttons down the front and the faux pearl necklace with matching earrings she'd picked up on her last visit to the Logan Antique Mall. She wore her red shoes, which gave the outfit a bright look. Viewing herself in her cheval bedroom mirror, she hoped Brent liked her appearance.

"What do you think, Ruthie, Penny? Does Mommy look good or

what?" She patted Ruthie and then Penny and headed for the bathroom to touch up her makeup, hair, and spray on perfume.

Five minutes later, she pulled out of the driveway and headed for the Logan movie theater to meet Brent. A pleasant glow of anticipation accompanied her as she drove toward town.

She hoped he looked forward to their second date, too. She'd had such fun on the first. Their dinner for two and the dancing that followed made her long for more. His effect on her emphasized her lack of male companionship. Besides, her biological clock kept ticking and nudged her to settle on someone, but not just anyone. Brent had everything she wanted—polished manners, confidence, and success. Now if he only enjoyed country living as much as she did.

When she reached the parking lot, disappointment struck. She didn't see him at first, but after parking and walking to the main theater entrance, she glimpsed him standing there looking as handsome as ever in dark blue tailored pants and a blazer. He waved to her.

"Hey there, Beautiful, I'm glad you could make it. What movie would you like to see?"

"Um, what do they have in a comedy?" She scanned the list of movies. "How about that one?" She pointed to a romantic comedy. She hoped she impressed him a little by remembering his movie preference.

"Sounds good to me. I've wanted to see that one."

He reached out, moved a wisp of her hair from her face, and tucked it behind her ear. Then his lips brushed her neck.

"Your perfume reminds me of a bouquet of roses." His touch flooded her senses with a pleasant glow.

He smiled at her as he took her hand and led her to the ticket counter where he purchased their tickets. Like a gentleman, he held the door for her.

"After you, mademoiselle."

Even his great French accent sounded perfect. Holding his hand made her body tingle all over, like riding a Ferris wheel. She liked the excitement and warmth of her hand in his.

"Why, thank you, kind sir." She laughed with him.

They approached the concession stand for popcorn and drinks before moving on to the ticket-taker. The young man tore the tickets and returned the stubs.

"You want the one just down the hall, first door on your right." He pointed.

"Thank you," Clarissa said.

She let Brent direct her to the right movie with his hand placed on the small of her back. Delicious waves emanated from where his hand rested. They grabbed two seats near the back. The smell of his cologne, like a grove of mountain spruce trees, enveloped her and made her dizzy with delight. Feeling giddy, like a young schoolgirl, she struggled to appear calm.

"It's much easier to get out at the end of the show by sitting near the back," Brent said. "Besides, I hate to crane my neck by sitting too close to the screen."

"Yes and it also doesn't disturb everyone else." She strained to maintain her composure. Get a grip, she told herself.

They started on the popcorn during the previews and opening credits. Once or twice, their fingers touched, sending chills up her arms and down her spine to make her knees weak. Brent smiled at her as if he experienced the same sensations. During the movie, he put his arm around her and drew her close. The scent of his expensive aftershave enchanted her.

Her thoughts drifted to David and their last encounter at the cafe. He had affected her with his casual relaxed attitude, and by how kind and considerate he was. Why couldn't she stop thinking about him? Even Brent's presence reminded her of David whenever he made her feel romantic.

Brent's solid presence reassured her, and, after a while, she rested her head on his shoulder. He held her hand and traced circles into her palm during the intimate, romantic scenes of the movie. Clarissa laughed several times during the funniest parts, and after the movie ended, the two of them left the theater arm in arm.

"Remember, we have dinner, too," Brent said as he helped her into her car. "Do you know the La Cascada Mexican Restaurant?"

"No, but I'm sure you do, so I'll follow you there."

They headed to the La Cascada for dinner and cocktails. On the drive there, Clarissa savored thoughts of Brent. Each time she saw him, she liked him more. He could be the one to spend a lifetime with and raise a family. She hoped he thought the same about her.

They met at the entrance to the restaurant, and Brent reached for her hand. "Ready for a romantic dinner for two?" His intimate tone enchanted her.

"Yes, I'm having a wonderful evening." Clarissa smiled at him, glad he appeared as if he enjoyed himself.

"Right this way," the hostess greeted them and led them to a booth near the bar. The low lighting created an intimate environment for them. Clarissa noticed that colorful piñatas and sombreros lined the walls, while maracas hung above the bar. The entire restaurant had rounded, arched doorways, and Mexican music played in the background. She even saw real cacti scattered throughout the place.

"Your server this evening is Donny, and he'll be right with you."

For a moment, Clarissa had thought the hostess said David. A mental picture of him popped into her mind—a tall, dark, handsome man in a suit eating blueberry pie. Forget him, she told herself and tried to erase the image from her mind. Brent deserved her full attention, not David, but the image stayed etched in the back of her mind. No, not David. *Donny.*

"Is something wrong?" Brent stared at her.

"No, nothing." She dismissed the incident with a wave of her hand.

He leaned across the table, and taking her by surprise, he kissed her with passion. The long, sweet kiss raised her temperature and sent her pulse racing. She broke it off to catch her breath.

"Where did you learn to kiss like that?"

"I've been kissing girls since grade school. The girls always liked my kisses, even then."

His superior look triggered annoyance. She disliked men who bragged about their successes with women, but grade-school girls didn't really count, she reminded herself.

She looked around the restaurant, fearful others might be watching them. A kiss like that shouldn't be for public consumption. Brent should have waited until they were alone, yet it was also exciting and stirred her senses.

"Umm, I see." Clarissa assumed she must appear inexperienced to a man who obviously knew exactly what effect he had on her. Still, kissing like that in a public restaurant didn't seem quite the thing.

"Hi, I'm Donny, and I'll be your server this evening. Can I start you off with drinks?" Their server set two glasses of ice water on the table.

The short, blond boy with brown eyes couldn't be more than twenty. He didn't have David's looks. How stupid of her to mishear the name.

"A bottle of your finest red wine, please." Brent spoke without hesitation. "Nothing less will do for my lovely lady." He winked at Clarissa.

"Yes, sir, I'll be right back with it and to take your orders."

Clarissa blushed and racked her brain for something to say to ease her sense of gaucheness. Nothing came to mind.

Brent reached for her hand. "You're something, lady. I've been looking for someone like you."

"Like me?"

"Ah, you're fishing for compliments. However, you're successful, focused, and beautiful."

His lavish compliment took her by surprise, but putting success first bothered her. Every woman liked being told she was pretty. She'd been called cute and even attractive. Being recognized for her business acumen was nice; she had worked hard to achieve it. Yet, did she want him to think that first about her?

"Uh, thank you." She fished for a suitable response, but she couldn't think of a snappy comeback.

"Here you go, sir, our best red wine." The waiter eased out the cork with care and poured them each a glass. "Are you ready to order, or would you like a few minutes?"

"We'll need a few minutes, thank you," Brent replied. "Here's to us, a match made in heaven, in my view."

He raised his glass and touched it to hers before taking a sip. His intense blue eyes held her gaze.

Yeah, trite, but maybe he meant they had a future together. Could he be for real? "I guess you're a romantic, but I'd say it's much too early to say that."

"Let's see…brains, business sense, and beauty. Word around town is that your business is doing well." His broad smile reminded her of a vulture hovering about its prey. "I also hear you have a beautiful piece of prime property."

The focus on money and possessions reinforced her alarm. "Guess the gossips are desperate for material. Yeah, I have a nice place. You'll have to visit sometime."

They smiled at each other as they surveyed the menu choices. Clarissa tried to keep her eyes off Brent long enough to decide on a selection. Not overly fond of Mexican food, she settled on a steak.

After they ordered, he again turned his attention to her. "So tell me more about *you*. What do you do when you're not working?"

"I work from home. I have a potbellied pig and basset hound. They're both so loveable and well behaved."

"You have a pig for a pet?" Brent looked at her as if she were crazy.

"Oh, yes, Ruthie is a Vietnamese potbellied pig, which means she'll always be small. She's highly intelligent, as are all pigs, a good judge of character, and very affectionate." Clarissa smiled with pride.

He looked slightly taken aback, but he smiled with effort. "Interesting. I've never met anyone with a pig for a pet. Aren't they always wallowing in mud?"

"Not Ruthie. She's cleaner than a dog or a cat. She's so smart and so sweet."

"Hmm, I um…look forward to meeting her and your puppy." He sipped his wine and stared at the other diners.

Clarissa wondered if he really meant that. The server returned with their meals, and they ate.

Finished, Brent sipped the remainder of his wine and eyed her over the rim of his glass. "Do you like fishing?"

"What? Uh, yes, but I don't go much anymore. I don't really have anyone to go with me. I've yet to make fishing friends here."

"Good. We should do that for a date while the weather is nice. We can make a picnic out of it." Brent reached across the table and grasped her hand. He squeezed it lightly and began to caress it.

His insistent touch stirred her senses. She liked being the object of his attention. Warmth permeated her body and began to bring pleasant images to mind. Could she get a high just from such a caress? Time slowed. She struggled to remember what he said last.

Fishing? Yes, fishing. That reminded her of her conversation about fishing with David. She could picture the two of them riding down the road on his motorcycle with tackle box and fishing poles. She smiled, lost in thought.

Brent squeezed her hand to draw her attention. "So, what do you say?"

She blinked. Somehow, she couldn't imagine Brent on a motorcycle. "Oh, um, yes, that sounds fine. It would be a perfect date."

Brent paid the waiter and took her by the arm. "Where to next?"

Her arm tingled and sent vibrations elsewhere. He led her to the parking lot of the restaurant and her car.

"Next?" Clarissa ventured to say.

"I could pick you up on our next date." His smile promised so much.

"I doubt you could find me. I live a bit out from town, and most people have trouble locating my road. Even with GPS, some deliverymen get lost."

"Why don't I follow you home tonight, and then I'd know where it is for our next date."

"Umm, I guess so."

This was their second date, and he hadn't shown any sinister signs. If anything, he acted a bit over the top, but she had a cell phone on speed dial for 9-1-1. Besides, she liked him a lot and wanted to move to see where things went. She suspected he'd be a great lover. He knew just which hot buttons to push. She only hoped she affected him as much as he did her.

* * * *

Brent drove behind her to her house, about five miles outside of Logan to a gravel country road lined with trees and open fields. They reached her driveway about five minutes after turning onto the gravel road, and he parked behind her car. As he got out, he stared at the gorgeous view of her home with a backdrop of trees and fields as far as the eye could see.

"It's breathtaking," he told her as he put his arm around her waist and drew her to him. The depths of his eyes fascinated her and promised so much. His strong arms encircled her, and his lips demanded a response. A long, hard, passionate kiss followed.

Brent's hands found their way to her waist, and he pulled her to him. He ignited an answering passion in her, and she kissed him back, exploring his mouth with hers and feeling his firm body pressing against her. It had been so long.

Chapter Eight
~ The New Girlfriend ~

Growing hot, Clarissa forced herself to break away from Brent's smothering embrace. Her lonely heart wanted him now, but her head reminded her it was much too soon. She didn't want him to consider her an easy lay. She wanted more from a relationship with him than that. Sex and passion would have to wait until she was certain he was the right man and not another Tony.

"What is it? Don't you want me as much as I want you?" Brent stared at her with confusion and hurt.

Clarissa gazed down, debating how to phrase her hesitation. No way would she rush into another relationship. Tony, her ex-boyfriend, had almost destroyed her with his infidelity.

"Uh, I've had a bad relationship and would rather take things slow, so we don't have any regrets."

"What regrets? We're perfect together, and I want you in the worst way. Surely, you can tell how you affect me?"

"I had a wonderful time tonight, and…I want to save something for our next date." She paused a moment, looking for a reason Brent would accept. "I'm tired and face a busy day of work tomorrow. I prefer to approach the next step when I'm fresh. Can I have a rain check?" She gave him a wistful smile.

"I guess I can live with that, but you drive a hard bargain, lady. How about I pick you up at six Friday night?"

"Great." Her lips brushed his cheek as she turned to open her door. "I promise to give you the grand tour of my home when you come on Friday."

He nodded. "I'm looking forward to it, so rest up. We have things to do."

His sly grin implied pleasures to come as he walked to his car and slid into the driver's seat. With a jaunty wave, he pulled out of the driveway. The car departed down the gravel road in a cloud of dust.

With a sigh, half-regretful and half-relieved, Clarissa entered the house to find Ruthie and Penny, tails wagging, waiting for her by the door. Ruthie gave little grunts as Clarissa scratched behind the perky ears, and Penny rolled over with her paws in the air.

Clarissa changed into some jeans and a T-shirt. "Hey, girls, how are you? I missed you both so much. How about a nighttime stroll?"

Walking would help restore her equilibrium. She grabbed Ruthie's harness and the leads. Ruthie waggled her tail and waited for Clarissa to hook up her harness while Penny, tongue lolling, jumped up and down. They set off down the two-lane gravel road in the sunset enjoying the fresh air and the gentle breeze. Trees and bushes covered the hills in the near distance.

A trail of orange flags ran along the side of the road. What on earth? Where did they come from? She was certain they weren't there this morning. Was the electric or telephone company installing some underground lines?

Off in the distance, wild dogs howled as the moon came into view and the sky grew steadily darker. Mindful of feral dogs, Clarissa turned toward home. She hated people who dumped unwanted animals along country roads in hopes they could fend for themselves, or some kind-hearted farmer would adopt them. It showed thoughtless stupidity. They had no heart and maybe no brains either. Too often, the farmer shot them because they preyed on livestock, endangering people, farm animals, and wildlife.

She had no desire to encounter a feral pack. "Guess we'd better head back."

At that moment, Ruthie squealed and hid behind Clarissa while Penny scrambled to cower behind Ruthie and Clarissa for comfort. A movement in the bushes frightened even Clarissa, but she couldn't imagine any large creature not making more noise or attacking without delay.

She took a deep breath and leaned down to pat them both. "It's okay, you two. It's probably just a rabbit or a possum." She took out her key chain with the pepper spray.

Then a creature about Penny's size sprang out of the bushes. Taken by surprise, Clarissa screamed and jumped back. Something soft and furry rubbed against her legs. She looked down to see Jasper twined about her ankles. He nosed Ruthie and Penny. Loud purring filled the air.

"Jasper, you scared us half to death. Go on, you silly cat."

She shooed Jasper away, but he followed them toward home, purring all the way. Clarissa stroked his soft fur despite her annoyance at the scare he'd given them.

"You're awful friendly for a big orange tomcat. You'd better go home before your master finds you missing." Ruthie grunted, indicating her discontent and jealousy, while Penny sniffed at Jasper.

"Don't worry, Ruthie, you'll always be my number one." She patted Ruthie on her backside and scratched between her ears to reassure her. "Penny, you're my second number one girl," she said as she rubbed the pup's belly. "You two will be best friends one day."

Chapter Nine
~ Cliff's Friend ~

Clarissa opened her eyes, greeting the morning sunshine and smiling as the memory of her fading dreams with David and Brent drifted away. It was Saturday morning. Tonight, she'd drive to Columbus to meet Cliff and discover his surprise, but first she had to do her weekly shopping.

She fed Ruthie and Penny, and then lingered over a cup of tea accompanied by a piece of her favorite apple crumb pie. Brent was a handsome catch. So why was she second-guessing herself over her feelings for him? He was smart, successful, and he liked her. He hadn't said anything to make her suspicious, yet she thought he was just a tad off in some way.

Why couldn't she stop thinking about David, her client? Somehow being her neighbor made distancing herself from him harder. He was a good doctor with a sense of humor, and he was kind with pets. Ruthie gobbled up her fresh fruit and pig pellets and waited by the door for their customary morning stroll while Penny wolfed down her dog food.

Sighing, Clarissa emptied her cup and placed her plate to soak in the sink. "Okay, girls, we'll take a quick walk, but then I have to shop." She walked Ruthie and Penny toward David's cabin, wondering if Jasper would be lurking nearby in the bushes. They encountered no sign of the cat this time or of David either. The cool, gentle breeze had cleared all but a few clouds. The forecast predicted a hot, humid day with only a slight chance of rain in the late afternoon or evening. Oddly disappointed David wasn't home, Clarissa started the return trek.

* * * *

Country folks shopped early, so by the time Clarissa reached the farmer's market, crowds of people picked over the dwindling selection of fresh fruits and vegetables. She selected a few firm late tomatoes and some lettuce from the first vendor she reached and placed them in her bag. She paid the man and moved on to the next table to buy blueberries and cantaloupes for Ruthie. That delicious piece of blueberry pie she'd shared with David came to mind along with David's beautiful smile whenever he looked at her. *Stop it, Clarissa*, she chided herself.

"Oh, Clarissa, how are you?" Donna Gilead, the real estate broker, called to her as she prepared to leave.

She swaggered up to Clarissa in a tight red skirt and silky black blouse showing a little too much cleavage. Her high heels made her list a little. Clarissa groaned inwardly, wondering what Donna could possibly want with her.

"I hear you're dating that handsome Brent Soulder, the stockbroker from Athens." Donna gave her a knowing look.

Meow! Clarissa forced a smile. "We went on our second date last night. He's a good dancer and so charming."

"Yes, I hear he's quite a catch. However did you manage to hook up with him?" Donna looked envious.

"I met him in the Logan Antique Mall about two weeks ago. He bought one of my more expensive pieces of Viking glassware."

"That's fascinating. I didn't know he collected glassware. He's such a hunk. All the women hope he might date one of them." Donna leaned closer. "Tell me, what's your secret?"

"Secret?" Clarissa drew back, startled. "I...I don't have one." Besides, she had no intention of answering such a rude question. "I hate to run, Donna, but I have to finish my shopping. I heard it might rain this afternoon, and I'd rather not get caught in it."

"I quite understand. I have errands myself. Well, good luck with Brent. Stop by the office sometime for lunch, my treat." Donna waved to Clarissa as she slipped away, looking disappointed and a bit suspicious.

That woman. She wore too much makeup, too much perfume, too much everything. Clarissa had no desire to encourage her.

* * * *

At Wal-Mart, moving through the store at a brisk pace, Clarissa pulled out her list and started adding stuff to her cart. She wouldn't count Donna as her favorite person, but as an astute businesswoman, Clarissa welcomed her envy of Brent. When with him, she worried his charm swamped her judgment. Finding such a great guy with fabulous looks and a successful career pleased her.

Finished at last, she smiled as she headed home from the store. Ruthie and Penny greeted her as she returned with an armful of groceries. "Looking for a treat? I bet you two smell the food."

Ruthie swished her tail while Penny licked her chops.

Clarissa put away the groceries and gave Ruthie a few blueberries and a bit of melon. She tossed Penny some dog treats and then fixed herself lunch. Even though it was Saturday, she had to finish some uncompleted billing and check her e-mail. The afternoon flew by and, before she knew it, she had to dress for dinner in Columbus with her brother. She took Ruthie and Penny for one last walk before leaving.

When they returned, she put on her favorite yellow dress with tiny red flowers and the red sandals that complemented the dress. Light, natural makeup, her hair pulled off her face with a clip, and a pair of gold earrings completed her outfit.

The drive to Columbus passed with thoughts of her brother and his recent success. As children, they had often squabbled. Thank heaven those days had passed. Only light traffic accompanied her.

She met up with her brother outside the Shogun Restaurant. He stood next to a young woman with Kewpie doll black hair and ivory skin. Her beautiful flowing dress decorated with Japanese-style flowers emphasized her Oriental air. Cliff looked his usual self in blue trousers and a button-down shirt in pale blue.

"Hey, Sis, what's up?" He smiled and waved to her as she approached. "I'd like you to meet Mieko, my girlfriend. We went to an arts festival a couple of months ago, and I got the best work of art there. You'll have to stop by sometime and see it."

A faint blush painted Mieko's ivory skin.

Clarissa hugged Cliff and then turned to Mieko. "It's a pleasure to meet you." She shook hands with the young woman.

Mieko's small delicate hands suited her ethereal air. She reminded

Clarissa of a fragile doll, or one of the beautiful drawings of a Japanese woman she had seen on the walls of a gallery. She envied that flawless skin and effortless grace.

"It's nice to meet you, too." Mieko spoke with a soft, sweet voice like a child's.

"Shall we?" Cliff opened the restaurant door and motioned for the two women to enter.

A kimono-clad hostess greeted them and led the three of them to a table where she handed each of them a menu. "Your server will be right with you."

"I love this restaurant, it's one of my favorites," Clarissa said as she looked around at the beautiful décor.

"Yes, it is beautiful. It reminds me of my home in Japan when I was little." Mieko smiled with a wistful look.

"How did the two of you meet?" Clarissa looked to Cliff.

"Mieko came to live here when she was ten. We met at the Japanese market when we both reached for the same package of edamame," Cliff answered.

"Oh, I see." Clarissa wanted to set Mieko at ease. "I bet it was interesting growing up in Japan."

"Yes, our culture is very structured and based on honored traditions. When we first came to America, it was a shock."

"I'll bet." Clarissa squeezed Mieko's hand.

"Hi, my name is Kaya, are you ready to order?" The dark-haired server stood with her pad ready.

"How about some edamame and goza to start with and green tea to drink," Cliff suggested.

"Sounds good to me," Clarissa responded and Mieko nodded in agreement.

"Domo, I'll bring your tea and place your dinner orders." Kaya headed for the kitchen, leaving them to peruse their menus.

Clarissa selected the sushi and shrimp tempura combo while Cliff and Mieko decided to share a sushi platter. The three of them chatted about American traditions versus Japanese and how commercialized the world had become everywhere. Cliff told her how he and Mieko were building a Japanese garden in his backyard so Mieko could have a taste of Japan.

"Your very own Japanese garden, how nice. Japanese gardens are so beautiful." Clarissa smiled as she thought about how nice it would be to have one of her own.

"What have you been up to lately, Sis?"

"Not much. I met a nice guy named Brent Soulder. He's a financial advisor and lives in Athens. We've been on a couple dates so far. I think I really like him."

"I'm happy for you. What kind of investments is he into?"

"Well, I'm not exactly sure yet...definitely the stock market."

"I'd be careful if I were you. Guys that play the market have big egos and are sometimes real wolves. I wouldn't want to see you get hurt. Something about that name sounds familiar to me." Cliff frowned as he contemplated it.

"Thanks, I will be. I certainly don't want another fiasco like Tony. Thank God, I didn't marry that one. Brent may have been in the newspaper as a result of his investments."

"Yeah, probably was. I read the paper every day."

"Say, have you heard of a company called Trade Industries?" Clarissa hoped he had.

"No, can't say that I have. Why?"

"The number that came up on my caller ID the other day—I've never seen it before."

"You should search the Internet, see what comes up," Cliff suggested.

"Yeah, thanks. I think I'll do that. It was probably a telemarketer."

The excellent food pleased Clarissa. She couldn't recall the last time she had sushi. Unfortunately, Logan had no Japanese restaurants or Japanese grocery stores. She often settled for Chinese food when her cravings got the better of her. At least those restaurants had tempura and pot stickers, much like goza.

Clarissa told them about how, according to Donna, women regarded Brent as a real catch. When they parted, Cliff told her to call him sometime next week.

Driven by impulse, Clarissa hugged Mieko. "I enjoyed meeting you. I can see why my brother's fond of you."

"Cliff is lucky to have a sister like you," Mieko responded.

* * * *

Clarissa devoted Sunday to her Vintage Wares business, updating her Excel inventory spreadsheet with the recent sales from her booth. She almost had enough pieces selected for her fall display and finished boxing up the selections for her next trip into Logan. She selected a nice piece she thought Brent might like and set it aside.

Monday morning, she felt on top of the world.

"I'll be back shortly, kids. I need to stop by the office and my booth, and then I'll spend the rest of the day with you." Ruthie grunted and rubbed up against Clarissa's leg while Penny just looked sad and rested her head between her paws.

On the trip to Logan, Clarissa passed a field full of deer grazing in the open pastures and it made her hear flutter with joy. How could anyone choose the city over a life in the country? As she neared town, Clarissa thought about Brent and how she liked him. So charming and distinguished, what more could a woman ask? She wondered what Cliff had read about him in the newspaper.

"Good morning, Clarissa," Geneva, Dr. Jenkin's receptionist, greeted her as she entered the office. "How was your weekend?"

"Delightful." Clarissa beamed at her. "Brent Soulder and I went to dinner and had a lovely time. I also had dinner with my brother Cliff in Columbus Saturday night and got to meet his lovely new Japanese girlfriend Mieko. She's a perfect match for my brother."

"Sounds great." Geneva paused a moment. "Uh, Clarissa, you might want to be careful when it comes to Brent."

"For heaven's sake, why?" She stared at her friend.

Geneva pursed her mouth, looked over shoulder, and leaned closer. "I've heard he's an investment shark. Rumor says he ripped off several people around here." She gazed at Clarissa with concern.

"Donna Gilead spoke highly of him." A frown creased Clarissa's forehead.

"Yeah, no doubt she would." Geneva snorted. "I thought you should know what people have been saying. Just be careful, I wouldn't want to see you get taken for a buggy ride or lose any money."

72

"Thanks, I'll keep it in mind." Clarissa frowned.

What Geneva said about Brent couldn't be true, could it? Brent showed such consideration and kindness each time they met. Geneva must have confused him with someone else, another investment counselor, not Brent. Clarissa put the thought out of her mind and focused on her work, exchanging chart documentation with Geneva and picking up the latest billing data. As she prepared to leave the office, David Claremont approached her.

"Clarissa, I'm glad I caught you. I hoped I might interest you in a concert Saturday. I'm playing as a guest in the Columbus Symphony Orchestra and thought you might like to come with me. It could be fun and give us a chance to talk over the practice. I'd like to learn a little more about our billing process so I can better document my patient visit information." He flashed a dazzling smile guaranteed to melt a heart of ice.

The Columbus Symphony Orchestra, she thought. *Impressive.* She hadn't been to a concert in far too long. Clarissa hesitated.

"Um, I'm not sure. Can I call you back and let you know after I check my calendar?"

"Sure, just let me know by Wednesday." He looked slightly disappointed and turned to go to his office.

"David," she called after him. "I'll let you know by tomorrow. I'd love the opportunity to hear you play in concert."

"Great, I hope your calendar is clear." His face brightened at her response.

Was he just happy about having someone to go with him or was it more than that? She felt butterflies in her stomach as she looked at him. A romantic relationship between the two of them would complicate things. How could she fall for a client? Was she?

She wanted things to remain professional. Besides, he said he wanted to learn about the billing process, so perhaps his motives were harmless after all. A concert would be a nice change and not really a date.

Chapter Ten
~ Just Desserts ~

Clarissa enjoyed the relaxing drive to the Logan Antique Mall to check on her booth and add some new pieces. A gentle breeze added to the mild sunny day and played with the few fluffy clouds dotting the sky. The pleasant day made her dread spending a lot of time on her computer when she returned home later. However, she could use her laptop and sit on the back porch to do her work while Ruthie and Penny chased each other around the yard. They would love such a gorgeous day.

Inside the mall, Brenda, a slender young girl with long blond hair like that of a model on one of those TV shampoo commercials, looked up as she entered. "Ms. Wilford, you have a check here for this month's sales. Things have picked up a bit from last month." She looked pleased as she held the check out for Clarissa.

"Thank you." Clarissa accepted the check and inventory sheet from her and looked to see what items sold. Someone had bought one of her most expensive pieces.

"Who bought this piece?" she asked pointing to the item listed on the sheet for one hundred fifty dollars.

"I don't know his name, but he sure was a hunk. I could get lost in those eyes of his. Good dresser, too." Brenda sighed. "Said he was new in town. Sure hope he comes back."

"Did he say anything else?" Curious as a ferret, Clarissa wondered if she knew the man and whether he would return. Brent had been here a number of times and wasn't new to town, so it couldn't be him. The only newcomer she knew was David Claremont. Could he be the buyer? What had he said over their lunch at the Café Corner? It was something about his mother collecting glassware.

"I'll ask him his name if he stops by again when I'm working," Brenda said.

"Great, I always like to know the names of my best customers." Clarissa turned away.

What did it matter if it was David? That changed nothing. If he had bought the piece, she could only assume he intended it as a gift for his mother. She had placed the expensive piece as the centerpiece of her display. The beautiful cranberry-colored bowl with a frosted crisscross pattern on it and fluted edges always caught browsers' eyes, but most people found it too costly. It would make a beautiful addition to someone's china cabinet. Pieces like that only appreciated over time. She hadn't brought any expensive new pieces with her so she would have to replace it next time she came to town. For now, she placed a moderately priced Fenton vase in its place.

Many collectors focused on Fenton, especially the painted pieces and those marked with the Fenton name. Too bad they didn't realize the value of the older pieces before Fenton added their logo. She had a few of the Fenton stretch glass pieces from the twenties and thirties in her own collection and treasured the beautiful shapes and iridescence of them.

Happy, she proceeded to add the new pieces and dusted everything. A neat booth with readable tags impressed browsers. The more she could tell them about a piece and its history, the more likely they would be to buy it, especially these days. The days of impulse purchases had evaporated.

On the drive home, her thoughts turned to the concert and her conflicting emotions about telling David she would attend with him. On the one hand, he was her boss and had spoken of wanting to discuss business with her. Yet she couldn't shake the impression he had more in mind than business when he looked at her with those hopeful green eyes. How could she control her undesirable attraction to him that made keeping the relationship on a professional level so difficult?

Dithering, she unlocked the door to find Ruthie and Penny, tails wagging. Ruthie greeted her with a series of happy grunts and squeals, anxious to see her and be taken on her midday walk. Penny jumped on her legs, begging to be petted.

"All right, girls, I know you've been cooped up all morning and you deserve your walk." Clarissa scooped Ruthie into her arms, kissed her on the nose, and cuddled her for a moment before setting her down and rubbing Penny behind the ears and on her plump belly.

She put the leash and harness on Ruthie. "Ready? Let's go."

Her thoughts returned to David with his winning smile and expressive eyes. He always made her feel special when she was with him. If only he wasn't her client. His behavior toward pigs, dogs, and cats made it likely he would make the perfect husband and father. *Stop it, Clarissa*, she scolded herself. *He's also hunter, remember.* Hunters kill animals and litter the landscape. Such a cruel sport had no justification.

* * * *

Donna spoke to her new clients, a youngish man and woman, about their desire to find a country home in the area where Jimmy, Clarissa, and David lived. Sizing them up, she liked what she saw. Tall and lean, Mr. Matheson wore his black hair and mustache well trimmed. His olive skin implied a Latino or Italian background. The woman, a Latin-American beauty, with long dark hair, green eyes, generous hips, and an hourglass figure resembled Jennifer Lopez.

The man's clothing looked expensive, and Donna thought his jacket had the sheen of silk. The woman wore a sheath that hugged her curves. Linen or raw silk, Donna guessed. A black BMW sat outside on the street. They smelled of money. Just the type of people a depressed community like Logan needed.

The man did most of the talking, and the woman nodded from time to time. He explained their desire for a prime piece of country property with extensive acreage. "You were recommended as the best realtor in the area," he said with a broad smile. "I'm sure you can find exactly what we want."

"Well, there's nothing on the market right now in this area."

She reviewed the properties in that area in her mind. David Claremont had just bought the old Jenkin place and wouldn't want to sell. Clarissa Wilford seemed unlikely to sell unless somehow that handsome Brent Soulder convinced her to move to Athens. So far, he hadn't done that.

Mr. Matheson frowned and looked at his wife. They started to rise.

Reluctant to see such profit go elsewhere, she scrambled for a response. "I can't think of a thing in that area except..." She paused. "Well, I know of one that I can research. The property's not currently on the market so I'll have to get back to you."

That prime piece of land Jimmy Johnson inherited when his father died would be perfect. Ten years ago, she had offered him a good price for his home and land, but he'd spurned the deal. He'd been a young man then, but with hard times and a growing family, she might persuade him for the right price. Surely, he wanted to do better by his family than that run-down farmhouse. If she offered him enough money, he'd take it. Mr. Matheson had money, and they specified the importance of the property location. A nice profit awaited her if she could deliver.

"Ms. Gilead, if there's even a chance they might sell, we're willing to wait. I'm sure you're persuasive. I'll make it worth your while." Mr. Matheson looked to the beauty with him.

She nodded. "Yes, we want that land," the woman agreed. "There is a nice profit in it for the seller and agent."

Donna gave them her best smile. "I'll stop by this afternoon and talk with Mr. Johnson. Perhaps, for the right price, he might change his mind. It's been years since he refused my last offer." She hoped he had mellowed and wasn't still the same mulish hothead he'd been then. "I'm sure I can reason with him."

* * * *

With the couple safely hooked, Donna drove to the Johnson place in hopes of finding Jimmy home and in a good mood. Last time she tried to talk him into selling, he practically threatened to shoot her with his shotgun. She pulled up in the Johnson driveway and smiled in relief when she spotted his ramshackle Buick. She'd hit it right, at least he appeared to be home. She could dangle the more than reasonable offer of ninety thousand dollars the Matheson's indicated they would pay for the house and land, double the offer she'd made ten years ago. As she walked up to the porch, she noted children's bicycles abandoned in the middle of the yard and the grass and weeds overgrowing everything. She tsked-tsked. Jimmy had no idea of how to take care of a place. Presentation made such a difference.

Clothes waved on a clothesline. Ragged jeans vied with torn T-shirts. Beyond the clothesline, the old barn looked worse than at her last visit and might collapse at any time. She'd have to get a crew out here to clean it up before showing it to the Matheson's.

Sighing, she climbed the sagging steps to the front porch, opened the screen door, and knocked three times on the heavy wooden door. A dog barked. Donna waited a full minute and then knocked again three more times and waited. Disgusted at the lack of response, she decided to stroll around the side of the house to the backyard.

As she rounded the corner of the house, she glimpsed Jimmy hoeing his garden. Her luck held and she had caught him alone. With his head down, he hadn't seen her.

Donna cleared her throat. "Ahem, Mr. Johnson, how are you this afternoon?"

Jimmy looked up and squinted. She stood at the end of a row of cabbages and put on her best smile.

"What do you want?" He eyed her with suspicion.

That didn't sound good. She hadn't even told him the offer yet. "Um, well, I came to share some fantastic news with you. A couple came by my office looking for a country farmhouse and said they would be willing to pay ninety thousand dollars for your place." She hoped he'd be staggered by the sum and wouldn't start yelling.

Jimmy scowled, but went on with his hoeing. "If I told you once, I've told you a million times, I ain't sellin' my place to you or anyone else. You real estate people are vultures."

"Oh, um, I hoped with the difficult economy you might feel differently. I'm sure the money would ease your situation and even provide for your family's future." Donna crossed her fingers and hoped the mention of his family would persuade him. "Why don't you want to sell?"

"Hell would freeze over first. This house and my land are the only things I have to leave my kids when I die. No one's going to change my mind no matter what the price. Do yourself a favor, leave and never come back."

The anger on his face scared her. No telling what a no-account like Jimmy might do. "Perhaps you should discuss it with your wife. This life can't be easy for her."

"Leave Ellen out of this. We're happy and don't need your meddling." Jimmy lifted his hoe and shook it at her. His vigorous shake dislodged a clod of dirt that flew toward Donna to land at her feet.

"I'm sorry you feel that way." She backed away. He obviously wasn't going to listen to her no matter what she had to say. This visit was a lost cause.

As she backed, her foot landed in something cold, wet, and squishy. Something icky slithered over her foot. She looked down to see a wiggling brown mass in a tin bucket.

"Yuck! What is this disgusting stuff?" A thin, single creature detached itself from the mass. "A worm? *Argh.*" With a shudder, she stumbled backward. "Ugh, get it off."

She shook her foot, but the bucket held her fast. With her foot stuck in the mess, she hobbled backward again. She gave her foot a vigorous shake, but the effort overbalanced her and she fell on her rump. Something soft and smelly cushioned her fall.

Dampness began to seep through her skirt. She put a hand down to steady herself, but it sank into a gooey mess. What god-awful mess had she landed in now?

An unpleasant odor engulfed her. She smelled it every spring when driving by Amish farms.

"Manure? Not manure."

She stared down at soft, greenish-brown stuff. Things couldn't get any worse.

Jimmy leaned on his hoe and burst out laughing.

"Don't stand there. Do something," Donna shouted.

She pushed at the bucket with her other foot and managed to dislodge it. Worms slithered from the bucket.

"Give me a hand, quick."

The bucket rolled away and landed in a nearby clump of weeds. Something black and white shot from the weeds and ran straight at Donna. An unholy stench filled the air. She pinched her nose closed.

"Skunk!" she screamed.

She rolled to the side, away from the fleeing creature. The skunk darted into the high grasses surrounding the farm.

Jimmy held a red handkerchief to his nose and looked about to burst. Tears ran from his eyes.

"Stop that. Stop laughing. You did this on purpose."

"No, ma'am, I wouldn't do that to my worst enemy. You can blame the worms and manure on me, but no one asked you to come or to step in that bucket. As for the poor skunk, no one controls them. I'll bet you scared the life out of that one."

Jimmy launched into another hearty laugh as he reached his hand out to help her up. "Guess Ms. Skunk thought you were going to fall on top of her." He grinned from ear to ear.

"This isn't funny, Mr. Johnson. You shouldn't leave a bucket in such an awkward place." Desperate and overcome by the combined stench of the worms, manure, and skunk, she grabbed his hand and pulled herself to her feet.

"How will I ever get rid of this…this awful stink? I can't go to my office this way."

"Well, you best take a bath in tomato juice. It's the only way I know to get rid of skunk stink." He looked about to start laughing again at any moment. "Anyway, the manure will wash off, but better do it quick before the stains set."

Furious he dared to laugh at her, Donna grabbed a clump of grass and tried to brush the back of her skirt. "I won't bother you again. People like you don't deserve good fortune." Fuming, she dropped the filthy grass and stormed toward her car.

"Hey, I'll get you a plastic bag to put over your seat so you won't stink up your car," Jimmy hollered after her.

Donna ignored him. She grabbed on old blanket out of the backseat of her car, climbed in, and sped off in a cloud of dust. How could that detestable man stand there laughing at her? The nerve of him! He deserved nothing from anyone.

* * * *

Clarissa struggled with the decision of whether or not she should call David and agree to attend his concert with him. She didn't have any plans for that day, but she didn't want David to misconstrue her acceptance as anything other than neighborliness, nor did she want to offend him because she had to work with him. His good looks only compounded the problem. Too, she had to consider Brent. They had only had two dates and he hadn't asked to date her exclusively, although she hoped things might move that way. Besides, David was a client, and she intended to keep things that way. So why was she feeling guilty at all?

Finally, she reminded herself that as a professional she could attend the concert for the benefit of maintaining good relations with her employer. She had too few opportunities to attend musical events in Columbus. However, she would not behave in any way that would mislead David as to her intentions. Tomorrow she would call him and tell him she would attend.

* * * *

When she called his office the next day, he answered on the second ring. She was surprised to hear his voice instead of Geneva.

"Hello, Dr. Claremont, I called to let you know I'll attend your concert Saturday." She paused, waiting for his reply.

"Wonderful, I'm glad you can make it. I'll pick you up at four, and we can have an early dinner in Columbus before the concert." He sounded pleased.

"Dinner and a concert?" Clarissa recovered from her momentary shock at the dinner invitation. "Uh, sure. I wouldn't miss the opportunity to hear you play." She'd wear something conservative and businesslike.

"I'll see you then," David said.

"Yes, see you Saturday at four." Clarissa hung up the phone to avoid further conversation.

What had she gotten herself into? Now she had committed herself to go and couldn't back out. At least Brent would never know since their dates were on Fridays and not Saturdays. Besides, it was just business, so why did she feel guilty?

Just then, the phone rang. Who on earth could be calling her? She didn't often get phone calls. "Hello?"

"Clarissa, darling, I'm so glad you're home." Brent's deep, sexy voice sounded on the other end of the phone line. "Listen, I was wondering if we could change our date from Friday to Saturday night instead."

The same night as David's concert. Oh God, what now? How could she tell him she couldn't go out with him Saturday without telling him about the concert with David? So what if she was going with David. It was a professional event with her client. *Go on, Clarissa*, she told herself, *just tell him the truth.* He'd understand. Wouldn't he?

Chapter Eleven
~ The Concert ~

"Uh, oh, I…"

Caught off guard, Clarissa paced as she sought a reason to tell Brent why she couldn't go out with him Saturday night. She didn't want to lie, but she also didn't want to upset him. She settled on a partial truth.

"Um, I can't 'cause…cause I'm having a business dinner with one of my clients that night."

"Oh, okay, I understand. I have to meet with clients for dinner occasionally too." Disappointment clouded his voice.

"If it's any consolation, I'd much rather be having dinner with you."

She hoped that would ease his disappointment. She couldn't mention the concert. Somehow, she sensed he'd consider the concert a bit more than business.

"Hey, how about we get together Sunday afternoon? We could grab a late lunch together. I'll pick you up at your place around one for lunch." Brent sounded pleased about his new plan.

His enthusiasm eased her worry. Besides, she wanted the opportunity to learn more about him as a person and understand what he really wanted in a woman. They hadn't discussed the future or anything serious except for investments. His questions about money still bothered her, but she reminded herself they were only natural because he was a financial advisor. His attentiveness and macho charm made her feel attractive and think about things she had suppressed for the last year or so. He made her feel like a desirable woman, something she hadn't felt since that jerk Tony had betrayed her.

How could she refuse?

"Okay, it's a deal. I'll see you Sunday at one. Did you have anything special in mind?"

"No, just a leisurely Sunday lunch so we can talk a bit."

"I'll be ready to go." This might give her a chance to discuss the rumors she'd heard from Geneva.

"Great! I'll pick you up Sunday. Later, babe." He disconnected before she could say anything else.

She'd wear something special, but casual.

Clarissa spent the next several hours submitting patient bills electronically and weeding through her overcrowded junk email. Finally, needing a break, she stretched her legs and rose.

"Come girls, it's time for our walk, and then we'll get some lunch. Let's eat on the back porch today so you can run around in the yard while I work on my painting." She hooked up Ruthie as Penny waited patiently. They headed down the drive for their usual walk. Ruthie nipped at Penny, and Penny barked at Ruthie. They chased each other side to side as if they were competing for leadership. Ruthie always won.

Off in the west, ominous clouds threatened rain. Maybe she should take an umbrella just in case. No, still plenty of sun and the walk wouldn't take too long. Besides, toting an umbrella made managing her two pets difficult. Too often Penny tangled around her feet.

Halfway through the walk it started to pour. She ran with Ruthie squealing and Penny running beside her. By the time they reached the front porch, they were all soaked to the bone. Looking at her pets and her wet jeans, Clarissa laughed.

"Gee, guys, I'm sorry. I didn't mean to get us all wet, but at least now, you won't need a bath. Let's go inside and dry off." She grabbed a towel from the bathroom and rubbed Ruthie and then Penny down until they were only damp.

"There you go, girls, all better."

After the passing rain shower had moved on, she spent the rest of the afternoon on her painting while Ruthie and Penny played together and chased birds. She stood back for a better view. Maybe she should add Penny to her painting somewhere, too.

When Clarissa looked back at her pets, she glimpsed Jasper teasing Ruthie by reaching his paw through the fence and tapping her rump. She laughed the first time she saw Jasper tap Ruthie and wondered what Ruthie would do. Another tap followed.

At first, Ruthie grunted and whirled around to see what touched her. She looked puzzled. Penny just watched and chewed on a bone. Jasper sat there, all innocence, grooming himself as if to say, "I didn't do it." Ruthie stared at him as if she considered him the culprit. It amused Clarissa to watch them.

* * * *

Clarissa spent Friday evening choosing her clothes for Saturday and Sunday and planning what dresses to wear. The concert required something dressy, but Sunday lunch with Brent would probably be more casual. Lots of families went to Bob Evans or Der Dutchman. She couldn't imagine any place romantic for lunch.

The day flew past. She had just finished dressing and had given Ruthie and Penny an early supper when David arrived to pick her up for the concert in the late afternoon. She hurried to open the door.

"Hello, come in and sit for a minute, please. I'll be ready in a jiffy."

She left him alone with her pets while she retreated to the bathroom for one final look in the mirror to check her makeup. A quick spray of her favorite perfume filled the air with the scent of lavender. On her return, she watched David talking to Ruthie.

David reached down and rubbed behind the little pig's ears. "Hey, little piggy, how's life treating you? You're so cute. I see why Clarissa loves you so much."

"Okay, I'm ready," Clarissa said, smiling.

David sniffed the air. "Mmmm, what's that perfume you're wearing?"

"It's called Lavender." She blushed as David looked at her with approving dark eyes. Compliments always disconcerted her, especially from a man who was also her client.

David's dark suit fit him well and emphasized his broad shoulders. Any woman would be proud to be seen with him. She picked up her purse, and the two of them headed out the front door. He opened the door of his silver-colored sedan for her, and she slid into the passenger seat. He leaned over her as he tucked part of her skirt inside the door before he closed it. She inhaled his clean, woodsy scent that lingered long after he shut her door. Daydreaming of the two of them surrounded by a meadow of wildflowers, Clarissa lost herself in thought.

How could she think of David this way when it was Brent she was dating? *Stop this!* she told herself, but her daydreams kept taking control. She struggled to turn her thoughts and conversation to more acceptable topics. On the drive to Columbus, they discussed the billing processes used in the medical profession.

"Proper documentation is vital to support accurate billing, especially for Medicare and insurance companies," Clarissa told him. She felt safer keeping the conversation on a business level. He appeared fascinated, although that increased her nervousness.

"I see. I'll make sure I take care in my records so your job is easier." David gazed at her with almost a look of awe. "I guess reading most doctors' scrawled notes must be difficult."

"Sometimes, but Doctor Jennings has never been a problem."

"I'll follow his example. After all, it's in our interests to keep the records so no one can argue with them." He gave her a broad smile that warmed her clear to her toes.

Worried his feelings for her might be more than professional, she vowed she wouldn't let him fall in love with her. She owed that to her business and to Doctor Jennings. She also had Brent to consider. She couldn't deal with more than one man at a time. Another suitor would complicate matters. David's attentions could only confuse things and might make their business relationship awkward.

Yet every time she glanced at him, her thoughts grew muddled. A tiny voice whispered she was falling for the handsome doctor, but she fought to convince herself it wasn't so, and in any event was unacceptable. Business relationships had no place for romance, and if that wasn't enough, he was a hunter. She reminded herself that she could never love a man who loved guns.

When they reached Columbus, David pulled into a familiar parking lot. Clarissa stared at the Shogun, her favorite Japanese restaurant, and then looked to David. His choice surprised her.

"Here we are. Have you been here before?"

"Are you kidding? This is one of my favorite restaurants." Clarissa grinned, pleased he had chosen this restaurant.

Other cars pulled into the parking lot as the dinner hour approached. The outside of the restaurant resembled a Japanese manor house with its wooden posts carved in intricate designs. It looked like something you would see featured in a guidebook for Japan. Its foreign air stood in sharp contrast to all the modern buildings in the area. Inside, a miniature Japanese garden with a small bridge led across a pond from the main entrance. Large goldfish swam in the water, and picturesque bonsai trees filled niches around the foyer.

"It's one of my favorites, too." David grinned at her. "I suppose next you'll tell me you love sushi."

Clarissa couldn't suppress her amusement. "Yeah, as a matter of fact I do."

"We can sit at the sushi bar and share a sushi boat for two, if you'd like. It isn't often I have a dinner companion who likes it, too."

"You've got a deal."

A petite Japanese hostess dressed in a kimono greeted them. At David's request, she led them to the sushi bar. "This way please. Ginger will be right with you."

They ordered the sushi boat for two and a couple of glasses of sake. Together, they watched the Japanese chef select, trim, and fix their entrée. Clarissa recognized tuna, salmon, yellowtail, eel, and mackerel.

"Here, try a bit of this." David came at her with a piece of sushi held in chopsticks.

She instinctively opened her mouth as he placed the offering on her tongue. It was mouthwatering. She had doubts as to the appropriateness of this gesture between two business partners; however, he was also her friend and neighbor.

"Very good. Here, it's your turn." Clarissa fed him a piece of hers and he responded.

They took turns feeding each other bites of sushi with chopsticks and sometimes fingers. Their efforts soon had them laughing. Feeding oneself with chopsticks offered a challenge by itself, let alone feeding someone else. Shifting a piece several times with chopsticks almost guaranteed it would disintegrate. Clarissa held her hand beneath the chopsticks to prevent losing any sushi.

One feeding attempt left David eating from her hand. She almost jerked back as his warm tongue and lips slid across her palm. Wanting nothing more than to savor his caress, she wished the moment would never end. Her eyes closed, imagining so much more. His tongue teased the center of her palm as he licked the sushi remains.

Fire filled her belly and stirred desire. Brent's kisses had never affected her so quickly or so deeply. Then David withdrew, leaving her bereft and wanting more.

She opened her eyes, but didn't dare look at him. Had it stirred him, too? Instead, she picked up her glass of sake and sipped it. Taking time to let it break the tension, she sighed before sneaking a side glance at David. A slight redness tinged his cheek.

"I love sushi and especially sharing it with you,' David said, his voice a trifle husky.

"Uh...yeah, I do, too." Clarissa paused. She definitely needed to cool down. "Uh, do you like green tea and ice cream?"

"Of course, it's one of my favorites."

"Let's have that and some green tea."

"Sounds perfect." David signaled the waitress and ordered.

The ice cream helped Clarissa to cool her emotions and establish a sense of normalcy again. While they sipped their tea, David explained his involvement with the Columbus Symphony Orchestra and how he came to train as a doctor.

"When I was a kid, my dad ran a corner grocery store. I think he hoped I would take over his business one day, but I disappointed him. I didn't follow his dream, but then he had my brother Ted to take over, so everything worked out well in the end."

David had never mentioned his family before. His face looked sad when he spoke of his father.

"Does your father still run the store with your brother?"

"My dad passed away about two years ago."

"I'm sorry, I didn't mean to pry." She cradled her cup of green tea in her hands and studied the surface, half-afraid to look at David. This conversation had become almost too personal. She needed distance.

"It's no problem. I like to remember him running the store. He used to give me and my brother free candy from the penny candy bin." His eyes crinkled as he smiled.

The conversation went well with discussions of their childhood memories and their favorite foods. He and his brother climbed trees and competed in track. Clarissa mentioned her brother Cliff and his new girlfriend.

"I use to write a lot of poems when I was younger. Almost have enough for a book." She smiled with pride.

"Wow, sounds like quite an accomplishment. You should get your poems published. I was never much of a writer. Instead, I developed a passion for medicine when I saw my dad do CPR one time. A man had a heart attack right in the store, and my dad restarted his heart before the ambulance arrived. I was amazed and decided from that day on I was going to be a doctor."

"Sounds like you were always ambitious. I bet your dad was proud of you." Clarissa instinctively placed her hand on top of his.

David smiled at her. "I'm sure he was."

She sat in silence for a moment, uncertain what to say. "My mother always encouraged my brother and me to set goals and make them a reality. I suspect my brother was a tad more successful than I was." She smiled ruefully.

"Looks to me like you've achieved a lot. You own your place and have a successful business. I'm surprised some smart man hasn't snapped you up."

"Hmm. That takes two. I almost got married once to a man named Tony. We were engaged and planning the wedding till I found out he was cheating on me. Now I'm not quite so trusting of men, and I'm more skeptical of love." Clarissa frowned as she remembered catching her cheating ex.

"I'm sorry to hear that. I had a girlfriend I thought about marrying, but we grew apart before I got around to asking her." David paused a moment.

"Clarissa, speaking of relationships," he said, "I heard you're seeing Brent Soulder. They say he's a savvy business investor, but I've heard rumors floating around about him that he's lost money for some of the elderly and their pensions." David's forehead wrinkled in multiple creases.

Annoyed, Clarissa's eyes widened, and she arched an eyebrow. No way would she discuss Brent with David. Anyway, who told him she was seeing Brent? Had Geneva?

"Your receptionist Geneva said something like that. I doubt you have any personal experience with him."

"No, I don't, but several of my patients have. I'd hate to see you involved with a swindler."

"The market's bad of late." Clarissa rushed to defend Brent. "You can't blame a broker for that."

"Maybe not, but I'd be careful if I were you and not invest any money with him."

David's earnest gaze unnerved her. "Look," she said tartly, "it's my business, not yours."

He had some nerve prying into her personal life. Besides, why did he care who she did or didn't date.

A sheepish grin crossed David's face. "Yeah, I know, but when I like people, I try to look out for their welfare. You're critical to our billing. As the new doctor in town, I'm anxious to see things run as well as have under Doc Jennings."

His words mollified her a bit. "I'm glad you think so, but I've seen nothing to support such a view of Brent. Besides, I never let my personal life interfere with my professional one." She emphasized her words as she crossed her arms and leaned to the side, anxious to end this politely.

Somehow, having dinner with her client and chatting with him like an old friend didn't quite fit her view of a business relationship. The conversation grew strained, and David tried to make jokes to lighten her mood, but heaviness hung in the air and increased the awkwardness.

"So, tell me about this concert of yours?" Clarissa wanted to move things between them to a more positive note.

"It starts in an hour so we'd better head to the theater." David smiled at her and signed for the bill.

He held out his arm to escort her to the car. Despite her annoyance with him for discussing Brent, she gave him a slight smile as she took his arm and let him lead her out of the restaurant. Silence filled the short drive to the theater. Had they run out of things to say, or was the awkward matter of Brent still on both their minds?

Clarissa wished the subject of Brent had never been brought up at all. They were really having a great time before that. Funny, how she felt so comfortable around David. What did that signify?

They arrived at the theater, and David came around to her side of the car to open the door. Clarissa stood and straightened her dress as David offered his arm and led her inside the theater.

The Ohio Theater held row after row of seats. Red velvet curtains trimmed in gold with heavy fringe and tassels hung on either side of the stage. Clarissa was impressed. Roman-style carvings etched the high cathedral-like ceiling, and a tall chandelier hung from the center. When the warning bell sounded, the crowds filled the seats in a flurry.

David escorted her to her seat. "I'll meet you in the lobby near the drinking fountain when the concert ends," he whispered in her ear and left to join the orchestra.

His warm breath left Clarissa stunned. Her ears burned like fire. How could he make her feel like this when she was so attracted to Brent? She blinked. What if it wasn't Brent, but rather the idea of a perfect life with a man she thought Brent to be? Maybe she was just desperate for a man, any man.

She struggled to regain control of her senses, but the tingling sensation lingered every time she remembered David's whisper in her ear or his touch on her hand. Did he know what effect he had on her? She hoped not. It would mislead him and take her down a road she had no desire to go—or did she?

The concert began slowly, growing louder in intensity as the music flowed through the entire theater and lulled the audience into a trance. They listened with breathless attention to the beautiful melody. The music carried Clarissa beyond herself and above petty concerns. Her eyes focused on David as he cradled his violin in strong, loving hands. She found herself fantasizing what those hands would do to the woman he loved.

When the concert ended and the applause stopped, she headed to the lobby to meet David. She glimpsed him by the exit talking with a stunning redhead. The woman, tall and slender, had curves in all the right places. Her hair resembled a lion's mane, full and cascading around her face. She leaned over and kissed David before leaving the theater.

Pangs of jealousy struck Clarissa like a knife.

What had gotten into her? Why should jealousy strike her when she already had the "perfect man"?

David approached her with a smile on his face. "What's the matter?" He looked puzzled.

"Nothing." Clarissa tried not to sound irritated, but the creases in her forehead made her look like she was frowning.

"I just ran into an old colleague of mine," David said. "Dr. Jillian and I went to medical school together. She graduated with her MD the same year I did."

Clarissa worried he sensed her upset. She hoped she wasn't that transparent.

"Oh, that redhead I saw you talking with a minute ago?" She wanted to sound cool and collected.

"Yes, that's her. She's working at Grant Medical Center here in Columbus."

"She's very pretty."

"Yes, but not as pretty as you." David grinned at her.

"Uh, thank you, but I'm just a country girl, nothing special." Clarissa blushed.

"Don't be so modest. You're more than that. You're a talented professional and a gorgeous woman with charm and charisma." He held his arm out to her. "Shall we go home now, Miss Wilford?"

She liked the way her name sounded when David said it. "Certainly, Dr. Claremont."

She grinned as she took his outstretched arm and let herself be led from the theater by the handsome doctor. Several women glanced at David with interest.

For a while, neither spoke much on the ride out of town, each occupied with their own thoughts. She glanced out the window at the disappearing city and then the welcoming country scenery that replaced it.

Clarissa decided to break the silence. "I enjoyed the concert and your performance. I've never known a violinist who played with such an august group."

"I'm glad you enjoyed it. You made our evening memorable as well, and sharing the sushi came as an unexpected treat. Few of my friends like it." He glanced over at her with a look filled with admiration and... "Perhaps we can do this again sometime?"

Clarissa nodded in response, but said nothing. She gazed out the window instead. Much as she had enjoyed the evening, if tonight was any indication of his effect on her, a repeat would be disastrous.

By the time they arrived at her place, her watch read eleven o'clock and exhaustion hit. "Thank you for the wonderful evening, David. I enjoyed the food and especially the fine music."

Stars filled the sky as David led her up the walkway and to her front door. Clarissa often stepped out on the porch late at night when she couldn't sleep just to gaze at the stars. They never shone as brightly in the city. A few fireflies glowed, stopped, and then glowed again, little flashing lights in the country night.

"I'm glad. I'll let you know the next time I have a concert."

He leaned over and his warm lips brushed her hand. Clarissa's palms grew sweaty. Warmth seeped from her hand up to her arm, and downward. She gently pulled her hand away. David drew back with a deep sigh.

She wanted to ease the awkwardness between them. "My poor Ruthie must be wondering where I've been all evening. I'll have to cuddle her and reassure her. She needs a lot of attention since Penny joined us." She reached for the door handle.

"Clarissa, wait," David reached for her arm. "I just wanted to say I think you're great, and I'm sorry if I offended you by my behavior at dinner tonight."

She sensed his guilt over the conversation about Brent, her boyfriend. Boyfriend? Only teens had boyfriends. How strange it sounded to think of Brent as her boyfriend, but he had become that, even if neither of them had actually used the term.

"Don't feel bad. Like you said earlier, you were only concerned about my well-being, and I appreciate that. Of course, your practice must take first place, and I'll do what I can to ensure the billing process functions well. As far as our first encounter, you were under a lot of stress with your moving into a new place and all."

"I'm glad you don't hold a grudge. I'll see you Monday at the office." He turned to go.

"David," she called after him.

He looked back at her with a sad look on his face.

"I, um, just wanted to say… I think you're great, too." She blushed, hopping she didn't come across as a silly schoolgirl with a crush.

"Thanks." He gave her a broad smile. "That means a lot to me."

His step appeared light as he got in his car and drove away without another word. Clarissa stared after him. Part of her wished he had kissed her lips instead of her hand. She couldn't help wondering what that might have been like. Well, it's probably better that didn't happen. Kissing her client was number one on her list of things not to do. Brent most certainly wouldn't like it either.

Chapter Twelve
~ Business or Pleasure ~

Clarissa watched David drive away and then entered her house. Ruthie greeted her with a snort and Penny with a bark. She yawned as she flipped on the lights.

"You missed me, guys. I missed you, too." She scooped up Ruthie and hugged her, rubbing behind her ears and under her chin. Then she set her down and stroked Penny's soft ears and belly. Opening the back door, she let them out in the yard for a few minutes before heading to the bathroom to prepare for bed.

"Let's hit the sack, girls, so we can get up early enough in the morning for our walk and a special Sunday brunch."

That night as Clarissa lay in bed, thoughts of David and Brent filled her head. Both men attracted her. Brent was everything she wanted in a man—charming, sophisticated, financially stable, and a hunk. However, David was also successful and handsome. Something about him made her yearn to be with him, but at the same time, she wanted to keep things on a professional basis without a romantic entanglement. Why was she even thinking of David like this when Brent was so perfect? She tried to push away such thoughts.

In her dreams that night, a nightmare with David threatening to shoot Brent with his shotgun horrified her. Only murderers shot other people. Though she couldn't remember why when she woke, she swore she'd *never* date David.

* * * *

Sunday came early. Anxious to see Brent again and clarify her feelings, Clarissa tumbled out of bed and headed for the bathroom. She pondered how to discuss the rumors she'd heard. She knew he could explain them. No way could she be with anyone who used the elderly like that. Looks and charm were great, but she wanted an honest, caring man.

Ruthie nudged her leg, reminding her of breakfast. She let the two animals out to potty while she prepared their food. She gave them each a special treat for Sunday. With brunch out of the way, Clarissa took Ruthie and Penny for their morning walk. As they headed down the road, Jasper jumped out of a nearby bush to join them on their leisurely walk. He rubbed against Clarissa and twined between her legs. She stroked his soft fur, and he purred loudly. Ruthie nudged her hand.

"It's okay, Ruthie, I love you, and no one could ever take your place." Clarissa patted her back.

When they reached David's cabin, she saw him sitting on the porch cleaning a gun. "Good morning," he called as she approached. "Nice day, isn't it." Jasper joined his owner on the porch.

Clarissa frowned at the gun as the memory of her unpleasant dream took hold. *It didn't happen*, she told herself. *Be civil.*

"It is. Are you hunting today?"

"No, I'm cleaning my shotgun so it doesn't rust." He smiled at her. "You have to keep your tools in top shape or they won't deliver when you need them."

Relieved he didn't plan to kill anything today, she wondered why he had to hunt at all. Men and their toys.

"I thought I might do a bit of fishing this afternoon. It's supposed to be pretty good this time of year."

"Oh? Where?" Now she remembered he liked fishing.

"Maybe Lake Logan or perhaps Stroud's Run. What do you think?"

"Both sound fine, but you might see a lot of people at Logan. It's popular with boaters." Pleased David was interested in her opinion, she turned toward home. "Have fun then. Bye."

A couple hours later, having finished some billing work and checking e-mails, she called Brent. Soon he would stop by for their quiet Sunday afternoon get-together. Just as she reached for the phone, it rang. She immediately recognized Brent's number on her caller ID.

"Hello, Brent. I was just getting ready to call you."

"Oh, I see. Did you have something fun in mind?" His mood sounded playful.

"Umm, I was just wondering if you remembered how to get here."

"You're a mind reader. I planned to ask you for directions and tell you to be ready at 12:30 sharp." His amused laughter came through the phone loud and clear.

"It's simple, really." She read him a simple set of directions and told him she'd see him soon.

"Sounds good to me." He broke the connection.

She replaced the receiver feeling elated at the thought of seeing him again. He would push David out of her mind. She jumped in the shower and then dressed, finishing in twenty minutes. After feeding Ruthie and Penny, she dabbed on her favorite perfume just as Brent pulled up in the driveway.

She locked the door behind her and walked to his car where he held the door open for her. He walked around to the driver's seat and smiled over at her.

"Where would you like to go for lunch? What do you think about that new Mexican restaurant in town?"

"Uh, I'm not that into Mexican-style food unless it's Taco Bell. My favorite kind of food is Chinese or Japanese."

She frowned at the thought of Mexican. About the only thing she liked in Mexican food were tacos, guacamole, or chile rellenos.

Brent frowned. "I'm not fond of Oriental food, so how about a compromise?"

"Sure, I know where there's an American-style restaurant called the Spotted Owl Café here in Logan. The food is pretty good, although I've only been there a couple of times."

"Sounds great. I like trying new restaurants."

Clarissa described the location of the restaurant. He drove there, arriving at Logan in record time. Brent did a double take when they entered, which made her smile.

She loved the rocky, fabricated waterfall with a fake white owl sitting at the top. Live plants spread out to frame the rushing water that cascaded over the fake rock formation. Other plants decorated various places throughout the restaurant. Beyond the waterfall, a big counter with a display case full of mouthwatering baked goods carried today's selections. The chalkboard menu on the wall above indicated sandwiches, burgers, salads, and soups.

"It's not quite what I expected," Brent said, not looking pleased.

"It's casual, but the desserts are superb. They're to die for."

"Ah, I thought the place might be a bit more…formal." He gazed around at the cafe again, frowning.

"A lot of the fancier places close on Sunday unless they're near the highway or it's tourist season. If you don't like this, we could go to Der Dutchman by the antique mall."

"No, you like the desserts." He sighed in resignation. "We'll stay."

Clarissa chose a salad, and Brent ordered a steak sandwich. He placed their orders, and they sat in a nearby booth. She took a deep breath. It was past time to learn more about Brent.

"So, tell me about yourself," she began. "You know more about me than I know about you."

He took a moment and studied her face. "Well, I was married once. We had one daughter; she's now fourteen."

Clarissa blinked, taken by surprise. "You have a wife and a child? What happened with that?"

Brent grimaced. "My wife was more interested in my checkbook than me, and my daughter became as selfish and self-centered as her mother." Bitterness filled his voice. "I don't do much business in Columbus, but I send cards and gifts at the appropriate times of year."

Sympathy for him made her reach for his hand. "That's terrible, Brent."

Divorced couples often tried to use their children against one another. His situation sounded like that might be the case. Yet, why had he said nothing positive about his daughter? Of course, teens could be a handful. He really hadn't said whether he divorced his wife or she sued him.

"Not really, it worked out for the best. Besides, my career doesn't leave much time for family life." He shrugged his shoulders.

Was he hurt so bad that he pretended he didn't care? She hoped he didn't still love his ex. "I guess things don't always work out the way we plan."

"You aren't after my money, are you?" He arched his eyebrows and grinned.

"Absolutely not." She smiled back, content with his response.

They finished the meal, and Brent took her hand as they headed out the door.

"I really had a good time this afternoon with you, David." Clarissa smiled, remembering the last meal she and David shared at the Shogun.

"What?" Brent frowned and raised an eyebrow at Clarissa in confusion. *"David?"*

"Uh, oh." Clarissa stared at Brent wanting to sink through the floor. His suspicious gaze at her warned her to say something. "David's one of my clients. Just the other day we had a business lunch, and this little place reminded me of it." Clarissa crossed her fingers.

"How nice." Brent studied her with narrowed eyes. "You're lucky to have such a good client." He studied her face a moment before smiling and relaxing.

Somehow, the smug look on his face made her wonder if he was laughing at her. He drove her home in silence, and they arrived back in her driveway in no time.

"I really can't stay," Brent said, "because I have some unfinished business that can't wait, but I'd like a rain check on that grand tour of your house."

Clarissa nodded, confused at his hot and then cold manner. He embraced her and covered her mouth with his. He proceeded to stun her with one of his intense, lingering kisses that made her burn from the inside out.

She broke it off before it led to more. She wasn't ready to jump in the sack with him yet, not after her last fiasco of a relationship. No, she wanted to take things slow this time and make sure he was the right one before embarking on such a major move in their relationship. She also wondered a little about his failed marriage.

He released his arms from around her waist. "I'll call you. Perhaps we can get together for lunch sometime this week."

"That would be nice." She turned and walked up the path to her house. He hadn't said dinner.

When she reached the front door, she watched the taillights of his car disappear over the hill. Her thoughts wandered. What would it be like to let go and find out how good a lover Brent might be? Yet, every time she fantasized about him, her thoughts drifted to David. Scolding herself, she tried to focus on the inappropriateness of a relationship with her client. How could she build a future with David? He killed animals for sport. What kind of compassionate man could look a deer in the eye and shoot it?

* * * *

On Monday, Clarissa entered the office full of joy. Things were going great with Brent. Soon she would bring him home to meet Ruthie and Penny, and perhaps they could become more intimate. That would end all thoughts of David.

She exchanged her weekly files for new ones and chatted with Geneva a minute. She turned to leave

"Oh, wait," Geneva said and grabbed Clarissa's arm. "Before I forget, David wanted to speak with you for a moment."

"Oh, what about?" She raised an eyebrow.

"Not sure, he didn't say. Have a seat, and I'll tell him you're here." Geneva picked up the phone to page David.

Clarissa sat in the waiting area and picked up a *Glamour* magazine just before David approached.

"Hello." He gazed down at her with his amazing smile. Why did a client have to be so attractive?

"Hello, Dr. Claremont." She struggled to suppress the butterflies that fluttered in her stomach. Her pulse raced. A client, she reminded herself, he's a client, nothing more. She simply had to keep things from getting too personal.

"David," he said and smiled again. "I hoped you'd join me for lunch today. I have something I need to ask you. We could visit Café Corner again for a piece of that blueberry pie. How about noon? Can you meet me there, that is, if you're not too busy?"

She paused a moment, wondering what he could possibly want to ask. Café Corner offered a public place, not an intimate, romantic lunch.

"Yes, I think I can do that. I have a few errands in town anyway, so I could meet you there for lunch."

"Great, I'll see you there then." He disappeared back into his office as Geneva ushered a patient into one of the examination rooms.

Clarissa stopped by the Logan Antique Mall to check on her booth and pay the monthly rental fee. Despite the recent sale of an expensive piece, if business didn't pick up soon, she might have to consider pulling out or relocating her merchandise. The slow economy affected everyone, and Logan suffered despite the tourist trade. Looking around and hoping to see Brent, she took her time finishing her business. Disappointed, she headed out the front door to her car.

Stopping by the local farmer's market, Clarissa picked out some fresh fruits and vegetables for Ruthie, Penny, and herself. The sweet scent of late peaches tickled her nose, and she placed one in her basket. Ruthie adored fresh fruit. A few apples, some bananas, and a cantaloupe completed her purchases.

"Hey, what's up," Jimmy hollered at her from behind his fruit and vegetable stand.

"Hi, I didn't know you sold produce here." Clarissa stared at him, surprised.

"Small world, isn't it?" He grinned from ear to ear.

"Yes, I guess it is. How are Ellen and the kids?" She surveyed his large selection of produce. He had some fine-looking tomatoes.

"They're all doin' fine. Little Jimmy's growin' bigger every day. I can't believe my babies ain't babies no more. They're growing up so fast." Jimmy looked a bit sad.

"Yes, I hear that a lot from people with kids. I guess that's the hard part of being a parent—letting your children grow up." Clarissa fingered some tomatoes.

"Ever plan on a family of yer own?"

"Sure, if I ever find the right man." She grinned at Jimmy.

"You will." He winked. "Could even be someone ya already know." His knowing smile hinted at something.

What did he know that she didn't? Did he have someone specific in mind? Most likely, he was just guessing. She couldn't imagine he knew Brent.

Clarissa bought a few tomatoes from Jimmy and said goodbye. She checked her watch and realized it was almost time to meet David. Not wanting to be late, she headed to the Café and decided to order a glass of milk while she waited his arrival.

The little café reminded her of a country inn. The checked curtains with ruffles and waitresses with gingham aprons added to the charm. As she studied the menu, she settled on a mushroom Swiss burger, complete with all the fixings, including fries. It had been awhile since she had a good old-fashioned burger, and restaurant burgers were much better than the fast food ones when they had that wonderful flame-broiled flavor. Burger King was the only fast food place that even came close to the taste.

"Hello, beautiful." David sat down at her table.

"What? Oh, hello." Had she heard him right? Had he said beautiful? Doubt shook her. He shouldn't use that word for a business associate.

"You haven't been waiting long, have you?"

"Oh no, not at all. I was reading the menu and admiring the atmosphere. I thought how good a burger with fries would taste right about now." Her mouth watered in anticipation.

"Sounds great, I'll have one of those, too." He grinned, showing his even white teeth.

The young server stood by the table and waited with his pad ready.

"Two of your burgers with fries, please," he told the server.

"Make mine a mushroom Swiss burger," Clarissa said.

"Sounds good," David said. "I'll have the same." He grinned at Clarissa.

"What would you like to drink, sir?"

"A cherry Coke please."

"Make mine a tall glass of white milk," Clarissa added. The server nodded and left.

"So, what do you want to ask me?" She didn't want a romantic entanglement with him. Besides, it would be considered unethical.

"Well," David paused a moment. "I have to take a business trip next week, and I need someone to care for Jasper while I'm gone. I hate to board him, and he hates it even more. He took weeks to get over it the last time I did. You live next door and Jasper knows you, so I thought maybe you could do us a favor, Jasper and me."

Ruthie and Penny liked Jasper and so did she. They would miss him if David boarded him. How could she possibly say no?

"Sure, I walk by your place practically every day."

She blushed, afraid of what he might think, but she always walked that way. Why did David affect her like this? She felt like a silly schoolgirl with a crush on her teacher.

"Great, I'll leave a key for you under the flowerpot on the back porch. Just make sure he has food and water once a day, preferably in the morning." He looked relieved. "Jasper will be glad. He hates disruption and likes Penny and Ruthie."

"Sounds easy enough." Clarissa smiled at him, but wanted to insure that her face didn't reflect any more than normal friendliness. Keep it professional, she reminded herself.

"Here are your drinks." The server set their drinks down in front of them, along with two sets of silverware. "Your burgers will be up shortly." He walked toward the kitchen.

Having settled the business of Jasper's care, David changed the subject. "So did you enjoy the concert last week? Would you like to try another one in the future?"

"Sure, that would be fun. I really enjoyed it, and you played so well." She sipped her milk. "Perhaps you'd come to a country music concert sometime." Damn, why did she say that?

"Sounds interesting, I like country. How's Ruthie doing?"

"Ruthie's doing well. She and Jasper seem to have become good friends. It's funny to see the two of them together, and Penny makes the mix even more amusing." Clarissa laughed at the thought. "They make quite a menagerie."

David laughed with her. "I'm glad to hear the animals are all getting along. I think Jasper likes having friends to visit, and now I know where to look when he runs off. How did you end up with Ruthie? I don't believe you've ever told me, and I'd like to know how you chose a pet pig."

"Well, a few years back my aunt gave Ruthie to me for a birthday present. I guess she thought a pig would be the perfect pet for me living out in the country. She knows I love unusual things and figured Ruthie would be just that. I fell in love with her that very first day when she looked up at me and wagged her little pink tail, snorting for me to pet her." Clarissa's eyes teared with emotion.

"Sounds like a smart animal. You're the first person I've met with one. I find that interesting." David's smile made Clarissa feel comfortable and warm.

"You know what they say about animals having a sense about people's character. I guess she knows Jasper and I are okay."

Just then, the server delivered their burgers. "Here you go. Two mushroom Swiss burgers with home-style fries." The server set the food in front of them.

Chapter Thirteen
~ Log Cabin Home ~

Clarissa's eyes got big. "This looks wonderful."

"Enjoy your lunch. Ketchup and steak sauce are on the table. If you need anything else, let me know."

Clarissa took a few bites and enjoyed the juicy meat with the fresh mushrooms. She sipped her milk. "So how are things going in your new practice?"

"Fine, Dr. Jennings teaches me a lot. Also, I'm getting used to this small town. I guess it grows on you after a while." David gave her a funny look and then tried to stifle a laugh.

"What's so amusing?" Clarissa frowned at him.

"I'm sorry, you reminded me of the 'got milk' commercial just now with that milk mustache." David smiled and held his finger across his upper lip.

Clarissa reached into her purse and pulled out her compact mirror. One glimpse and she quickly wiped her face. As she looked over at David, she laughed, too.

"I guess I looked pretty silly with milk on my face."

At that moment, the server approached their table. "How is everything? Can I get you folks anything else?"

"No, we're fine for now, but we'll want one piece of blueberry pie with two plates for dessert later," David told her.

"Okay, I'll check later and bring your dessert. Would either of you like more to drink?" She waited a moment.

Clarissa looked to see both their drinks were still half full. "No thanks, we're fine." The server left them to stop at another table.

David smiled. "I've enjoyed this lunch with you. We should do this at least once a week. What do you think?"

Clarissa had to admit she found the food delicious, and David made pleasant company. "Sounds fine. I can update you on my work, and you can ask me any billing questions you have."

She hoped he'd understand she wanted to keep things on a professional, but friendly level. David looked disappointed and even a little hurt. She hadn't wanted to offend him.

He nodded. "Okay, how about every Monday at noon?"

"Sure, eating here once a week with you would suit me."

The thought of seeing David more often pleased her, since she found him so hard to resist. As a new person in town, he wanted to make friends, and she knew a lot about the community.

She bit into the juicy burger. "This is delicious. How's yours?"

"Great. I think I'll order more burgers here in the future, say every Monday." He grinned at her.

The two of them finished their meal and shared a slice of blueberry pie with vanilla ice cream. Clarissa savored every bite.

"I'm glad you recommended this."

"Thank Donna, she dragged me to the town festival, and I sampled it there. I had hoped to see you there."

"Uh, no I had a date that night." His disappointed look surprised her.

"I hate to eat and run, but I have a full schedule this afternoon," he said. "And I am sure you have a lot to do, too."

"Yeah, I should get going."

"I'll call you before I leave next Monday to go over any final details related to Jasper before I head out of town. I appreciate you doing this favor for me. I don't know anyone else to ask, and you do live right next door."

"It's no problem, really. I'm happy to take care of Jasper. He's quite a cat."

"That he is." A smile lit up his face.

He must love that cat. Lucky Jasper.

* * * *

The two of them parted ways, David heading back to his office, and

Clarissa to the local Wal-Mart. At Wal-Mart, she ran into Donna, the real estate woman.

"Clarissa, darling, how are you? How are things with that handsome Brent Soulder?" Donna looked envious.

"Well, he's charming."

"You wouldn't be the first woman to be swept off her feet by that man." Donna gazed at her with a knowing look.

"I wouldn't know about that, but he definitely has potential."

Donna glanced at the bag of dog food in Clarissa's shopping cart. "I thought you had a pig?"

"I do, but one night when I came home after a date with Brent, I found a little basset hound pup on my doorstep. I couldn't find her a home, so I adopted her and she's been with me ever since." Clarissa smiled as she thought of playful Penny with her big ears and sad eyes.

"A stray?" Donna sniffed. "My Cuddles is a pedigreed miniature poodle. Her mother and sire won awards in the major dog shows." Her hoity-toity attitude annoyed Clarissa. "Has Brent met the pig yet?"

"Uh no, but he will soon. We enjoy spending time together, and I'm sure he'll love my pets, too." Clarissa spoke with confidence. Who wouldn't love Ruthie and Penny?

"Perhaps if you and Brent moved in together, you might consider selling your place. I have some buyers who are willing to pay good money for properties in your area."

Donna's sly look made Clarissa narrow her eyes. What was the woman up to?

"Absolutely not! I'd never sell my little place." Clarissa tried to contain her anger. "Do you know anything about the orange flags alongside the road out my way?" She eyed Donna with suspicion.

"Orange flags?" Donna appeared puzzled. "No, I can't say I do."

Clarissa arched an eyebrow. "Oh? My best guess is a work crew is planning some underground cable installation."

Her annoyance with Donna spurred her curiosity. She couldn't imagine Donna not knowing all the happenings in the area. Maybe someone else knew.

"I have to go," Clarissa said. "If I don't get home soon, my pets will be chomping at the bit."

"Yes, I have to get back to the office. I have some clients stopping by this afternoon. It was good to see you. Say hello to your new beau." Donna left Clarissa to her shopping.

After going through the checkout, Clarissa headed for home. She thought about how much she loved Ruthie and Penny and enjoyed their company, but it would be nice if *Mr. Right* would come along before she grew too old to have a family. She wondered how long it would be before she had children of her own.

She envied Jimmy his children. It was amazing how with so little, he took good care of his family. Being unmarried wasn't bad, but her desire for a family had grown with her move to the country. However, she had met few men who measured up to her standards. Now she knew two, but one had to remain off-limits. Luckily, Brent could be the man to make her life complete.

The week flew past. Sunday, Clarissa remembered David would be leaving on his trip. Later that morning he called her.

"Hello, Clarissa. I was hoping you could stop by for a few minutes so I can give you all the necessary information and a key to the back door. I have to leave first thing in the morning and don't want to disturb you that early."

"Sure, okay if I bring Ruthie and Penny along? We were just getting ready for a walk."

"Yes, they're always welcome around my place. See you soon."

Clarissa hung up and headed out the door with Ruthie and Penny for their walk. She reached down and stroked her pig on the top of her nose. Ruthie loved to have her snout rubbed there. Penny danced about for her share of attention.

"You sweet little thing, you." She patted Penny's side. "What am I going to do with you?"

Heading up the hill toward David's place, Clarissa thought about her feelings for him. She found him a kind and considerate man. However, she mustn't let herself be swayed by that. *Guns, hunting, killing.* She hugged those words to herself like armor.

"Hello, enjoying your stroll I hope." David smiled at her from his porch where he sat with Jasper cleaning that cursed gun of his again.

His words startled her because she had been focused on her thoughts and hadn't realized she'd reached his place so soon. She'd walked a mile and not even known it. At least she never had to worry about her weight as long as she walked Ruthie and Penny.

"It's a beautiful day, isn't it? I guess today is my lucky day. I get to see inside your log cabin. Old Man Jenkin always kept to himself. Folks called him a hermit."

"It's not much compared to big houses in the city, but it feels like home to me and Jasper. It did take quite a bit of elbow grease to clean it." Jasper rubbed up against David's leg at the mention of his name.

"Let's show them around, Jasper." He reached down to pat Ruthie on the back. She rubbed up against his leg just like Jasper had done. Penny laid her head down at David's feet.

"Aren't you the friendliest little pup?" He rubbed behind her big ears and chuckled.

Clarissa followed David into the house with Ruthie, Penny, and Jasper following close behind. The low ceiling painted light blue reminded her of the sky outside. An oak board, with a row of six pegs on the wall by door, provided a place for coats. The living room lay to the right of the entrance, and the large brick fireplace drew the eye. A black fire screen around the base protected the carpet and a large box next to the fireplace contained chopped pieces of firewood. She liked the dark green sofa and matching recliner before the fireplace and the simple wood coffee table in front of the sofa.

"You have a lovely home. Did you decorate it yourself?" She gazed at the plain but comfortable room. She admired the simplicity of his style.

"Yes, I did. I used *Country Living Magazine* for ideas."

"Well, you did a fantastic job. Who's the little girl in the painting?" Clarissa gestured toward the large painting over the fireplace above the mantle, portraying a little dark-haired girl burying her nose in a handful of flowers. Purple, orange, and yellow wildflowers filled the meadow behind her.

"I bought that in Columbus at an art gallery last year. It appealed to me, and if I ever have a little girl, someday I want her to enjoy nature."

The thought of a family made Clarissa blush. "It's lovely. I'm sure you'll find a good woman to marry and have a family with you, including a little girl." Why did David have be a man after her own heart?

"Yes, maybe sooner rather than later." He smiled as if he knew a secret.

Disappointment hit her. Maybe she had misread his interest, and he had a girlfriend—maybe that lady doctor they met at the concert.

"The kitchen is this way." He led her down the short hallway to an open area. Large oak cabinets lined the walls and a round table with four chairs filled the center of the room.

Jasper rubbed up against Ruthie and purred loudly. Ruthie snorted, but didn't shy away or avoid Jasper. Penny tried to chew on Jasper's tail, but the cat whipped around too quickly. Startled, Penny sat down and whined. Ruthie started licking Penny like a kitten needing a bath.

"This is a lovely house, inside and out. Do you mind if I ask how much you paid for it? Curiosity is killing me."

"Sure, I don't mind. I actually got a real good deal on the place. Sixty-five thousand, because of the condition in which Jenkin left it. I couldn't pass it up, not to mention the view of the countryside. Best investment I've ever made."

"I paid a little more than seventy thousand for my piece of serenity, but property values around here keep rising, especially with the Lancaster bypass."

"This door leads outside." David walked over and pointed to the small pet door built into it. "Jasper pretty much comes and goes as he pleases, except at night when I lock him up to protect him from wild animals. He always wakes me around seven in the morning to let him out. He has the litter box for nighttime." He pointed next to the back door.

"That's pretty neat. Maybe I should consider installing a pet door for Ruthie and Penny. My backyard is fenced. We'd still take our daily walks, of course." She grinned at him. "I need my exercise."

"I keep the cat food in this cabinet." David opened up one of the lower cabinets. "I usually feed him canned cat food in the morning and leave a bowl of dry cat food to last him the rest of the day. You would only need to come over twice a day, once in the morning to feed him and open the pet door, and once in the evening to shut him in for the night."

Ruthie and Penny both looked on with interest and sniffed the air as the scent of food drifted their way. Jasper sat at attention.

"Sounds easy enough. What if I need to reach you for some reason?"

"My number is here on the fridge. I've included my cell phone and the second number is the hotel where I'm staying." He pointed out the list to her.

"Great, it sounds like I have all the information I need." Clarissa turned ready to leave.

"How about joining me for a cup of coffee on the front porch? I often see deer grazing in the field across the road this time of day." He poured himself a cup of coffee.

He appeared sincere and part of her wanted to stay and spend more time with him. She felt at odds with herself, especially the part of her that would miss him while he was gone. She needed to distance herself and settle her mixed emotions. Besides, there was Dr. Jillian. She might be David's girlfriend.

Still, coffee wasn't romantic. They were neighbors as well as business colleagues. He might misunderstand if she refused his friendly overture so, despite her better judgment, she accepted.

"I'm not a coffee drinker. Do you have tea instead?"

"Well, you'll be happy to know I do keep some tea on hand for guests. A penny for your thoughts?" David looked at her, one eyebrow raised.

"Oh, um." Clarissa snapped out of her imaginings, only now aware she had drifted off. "I was thinking about how pleasant it is living out here and seeing deer in my backyard almost every day." She crossed her fingers and hoped David didn't suspect her real thoughts about him or Dr. Jillian.

He fixed her a cup of hot tea using the microwave. "Cream or sugar?"

Suddenly, a large spider crawled across the floor. Clarissa screamed and scrambled backward, tripping over a rug and landing on her backside. David smashed it with his shoe and helped her back on her feet.

"I take it you and spiders don't get along." David looked at her with laughter in his eyes.

"No, I am most definitely afraid of them. All creepy-crawly things really freak me out." She turned up her nose at the dead spider as David took a paper towel and cleaned it up.

"Here." David handed her the cup of tea and led her to the front porch. "Shall we?"

She accepted the tea and took a sip. It soothed her nerves at once.

"If we do see deer, I have binoculars we can use to get a closer look without frightening them away." He reached into a drawer in the hallway table to pull them out.

On the porch, seated in comfortable wicker chairs, they sipped their hot drinks in silence. Ruthie lay down at Clarissa's feet while Jasper curled up beside her, and Penny lay beside Jasper. The three of them made quite a sight. Clarissa turned her attention toward the woods. Just when she thought they wouldn't see anything, a small herd of the shy creatures emerged.

No hunters lurked nearby as she spotted one buck accompanied by four doe. David raised his binoculars. With caution, he handed them to Clarissa. She stared as the deer grazed in the field. Why hadn't she thought about getting a pair of binoculars before? Seeing these delicate creatures so close filled her with admiration, and she almost forgot to breathe. Bird watching was one thing, but this... The sight of such peaceful animals overwhelmed her.

When she finally pulled the binoculars away from her face, she found David staring at her in a way that made her blush from the inside out. His intense gaze made her heart flutter. Why did he have to be her client? His gaze implied he found her fascinating.

"I really must go. I have to tie up some loose ends before tomorrow morning and check my e-mail." Clarissa hoped David would see this as a good enough excuse for her to leave. The longer she stayed, the more uncomfortable she grew.

"Yeah, I've some last-minute things myself before tomorrow. I leave early."

With that, Clarissa and Ruthie set off home with Penny at their heels. She hoped her face didn't reveal what she felt. Did David realize what he did to her? Probably not. If she had stayed any longer, what would have happened? It was obvious David was interested in her on more than a professional level. For that matter, she was attracted to him too. She could feel it, like a big magnet pulling at her as she tried to run the other way. How long could she resist the natural urge to run into his arms? Scarlet O'Hara wouldn't hesitate.

Chapter Fourteen
~ The Unexpected Visitor ~

The next morning Clarissa headed toward David's place to feed Jasper and open his cat door for the day. Penny and Ruthie walked alongside her, playing as they traveled the gravel road. Penny nipped at Ruthie's tail and Ruthie nipped back, snorting and nudging Penny in the side.

"Stop that, you two. You'll trip me and make me skin my knees. Lord knows I'd fall flat on my face."

Inside David's cabin, Jasper mewed, anxious for his breakfast. He wanted to get outside for the day to whatever mischief he could find. Probably kill a mouse or bird. Everyone considered cats first-class hunters.

She hooked Ruthie's lead to one of the wooden rails on the back steps. "You and Penny behave while I tend to Jasper, and I'll give you both a treat when we get home."

Satisfied they would be all right for a few minutes, she went inside. Jasper immediately rubbed up against her leg as she opened the cabinet door to fetch his food.

"Meow." Purring loudly, he followed her over to his food dish and watched while she put some wet and then dry cat food in his bowl next to his water.

"There you go, Jasper, enjoy. Your daddy is lucky; you're such a handsome cat." She stroked him a few times, then opened the pet door, locked the back door behind her, and headed home with her frisky pets.

After breakfast, she gathered up her completed patient files to exchange for more work at the office and headed out the door.

* * * *

"Good morning, Clarissa." Geneva smiled at her from behind the receptionist's desk. "I hear from Donna things are getting serious between you and Brent."

"Donna would say that, but we need more time to get to know one another." She swapped her old patient files for new ones. "Did you know he was married before and has a fourteen-year-old daughter?"

"No, I didn't." Geneva looked surprised. "What did he have to say about that?"

"Just that the marriage didn't work out because his wife was a gold digger. He spent lots of time in the office due to demands of his work. His ex lives in Columbus and he sends cards and presents to his daughter since his business doesn't allow him the opportunity to get there too often."

She omitted the part about his daughter being like her mother in hopes her response satisfied Geneva's curiosity.

A patient arrived and Geneva had to tend to her before she could continue the conversation about Brent. Not wanting to discuss her relationship with him any further, Clarissa hurried to gather her patient files for the week and bade Geneva a quick good-bye as she slipped out of the office.

As she completed a few errands and did a bit of shopping, her thoughts turned to David. She was disappointed they wouldn't have lunch together at the Café Corner this week. Even though they were client and contractor, she still enjoyed their times together. They shared a number of interests like their love of music, the country life, and of course devotion to their pets.

* * * *

Later that evening, she headed to David's place to check on Jasper and close the cat door for the night. She left Ruthie and Penny home this time. Jasper sat before the cat door and meowed in a loud voice. Clarissa wondered why he hadn't gone inside.

She opened the back door of David's house and stopped. "Oh, my God!

She stared at the strangest and funniest sight she'd ever seen. No wonder Jasper wouldn't go inside. A ring-tailed creature sat on the kitchen countertop beneath an open cabinet munching on a cracker, with his head covered in flour. Her entrance startled him, and he turned to stare at her with beady little eyes. Flour covered his face and paws. He ran, leaving a trail of floury paw prints across the countertops.

She laughed so hard she thought her sides would burst. What a ridiculous sight. If only she had a camera. Jasper, close by Clarissa, growled, but stayed behind her.

Beneath the flour, Clarissa recognized a raccoon, his mask partly obscured. The startled creature scrambled down onto the floor.

She reached for a broom and used it to try to shoo the critter out the back door she had propped open. The coon raced around the kitchen like its tail was on fire, dodging Clarissa's broom and knocking more things over. It twisted through the mess littering the floor, first right, then left, dodging the swinging broom. Then she skidded and almost tripped. Only a grab at the table saved her from landing on her rump.

No way would this animal get the better of her. With renewed determination, she swung her broom in wide arcs, but failed to touch the creature. She gasped with frustration. Winded, she had to stop for a moment to catch her breath.

Panting, she stared at the raccoon. "You're going out!"

She raised the broom, but the animal ducked and came up on the other side. That only made Clarissa swing at it with more vigor. She succeeded in chasing it back across the kitchen where it jumped into an open cabinet door. Clarissa poked inside with her broom and heard a snarling sound.

The creature refused to cooperate. It wouldn't be easy to evict it from David's house. What would he say if he came home to find this rascal living in his kitchen?

How could she get it out? She'd have to clean the kitchen and keep the animal from returning. Moreover, what would she do about Jasper? He'd have to stay with her until David came home.

At a loss for what to do, she plopped down on a nearby chair. Who would know about raccoons?

Jimmy! Why didn't she think of him before? He trapped annoying animals for a living. She rummaged through the closest for a phone book and thumbed the pages. *Johnson, Jimmy*. She dialed the number and prayed he'd be home.

His wife answered after the fourth ring. "Hello, Ellen speaking."

"Hi, Ellen, this is Clarissa. I wondered if your husband was home. I have a critter problem and hoped he could help." Clarissa drummed her nails on the counter as she waited. What if he wasn't home?

"Sure, he's here. Just a minute and I'll get him for you. What kind of critter is it?"

"Um, a raccoon, he's wreaking havoc inside Dr. Claremont's cupboards and I can't get him to leave." Desperation colored Clarissa's voice.

Ellen laughed at Clarissa's description. "That's a problem. Don't worry, Jimmy can trap anything. I'll get him right away."

A minute later Jimmy's voice came over the phone. "I hear you have a bit of a raccoon problem at David's house. I'll be there in about twenty minutes to set a trap. We'll have him caught by morning."

"Thank you, Jimmy, you don't know how grateful I am." Clarissa sighed with relief and agitation. "I don't know what I'd do if I hadn't thought to call you. I tried to shoo him out with a broom, but he only retreated into the cupboard and then he snarled at me."

"You might be better off to wait outside till I get there. Coons sometimes get rabies and are more vicious than people realize. You wouldn't want it to bite you."

"Sure, no problem! He may be cute, but after that nasty snarl I don't want to get too close or irritate him anymore than I already have."

She waited outside with Jasper for Jimmy to arrive. David was due back in a couple of days. Clarissa wanted to have his house clean for him when he arrived, and finding a raccoon in his kitchen wouldn't be a good thing at all.

About twenty minutes later, Jimmy arrived as promised with a cage. "Don't worry. I've captured lots of 'coons in my time and never got bit once."

He entered the house, set the trap in the middle of the floor, and placed some slices of apple with peanut butter inside the trap. "Any newspaper?"

"Newspaper?"

"For under the trap. They can make a big mess."

"Oh, yeah, I remember seeing some next to the fireplace." She hurried off and returned with a handful of papers.

"I could pay you something for doing this." Clarissa handed him a stack of old newspapers.

"No, that's okay. We're neighbors. Besides, David is my good buddy."

Jimmy spread newspaper in several layers beneath the cage. "I'll check the trap first thing in the morning and haul your raccoon away, with any luck." He smiled and bid Clarissa a good evening leaving her with Jasper.

Clarissa gathered up Jasper's bowls and cat food. "Here, kitty, kitty," she called to the cat. "I'm afraid you're stuck with me till your daddy comes home." She reached down and stroked Jasper's soft orange fur. A loud purr answered her. She gently picked him up and placed him in her car.

Ruthie and Penny greeted Jasper with grunts and licks. Jasper seemed content to join them and settled on a nearby chair for a nap. Clarissa set up the cat's bowls with food and water on the dryer in the laundry room to keep Ruthie and Penny from getting in his food. Next, she fixed dinner for all of them.

What would David think when she told him the story? What a mess the raccoon had made and was probably still making. She hoped she could get everything cleaned up by the time he got back. Clarissa would warn him about the open cat door.

Clearing away her dinner dishes, she went outside to watch the sun set over the trees. As she watched the beautiful purple and orange hues in the darkening sky, her thoughts turned to Brent and their last date. He'd said some disturbing things about his past and about himself, things she didn't like at all. After her last boyfriend, Tony, had burned her with lies while letting her believe she was the only one for him, she remained suspicious and determined to be careful.

She cautioned herself not to be overly critical and wary of Brent, because he was a different person than Tony and deserved her trust and respect as an individual. She would not tarnish this relationship with memories of the past. She smiled to herself. Brent's charm and his aura of assurance made him so attractive, and he acted as fascinated by her as she was by him. However, as their relationship grew more intense, sexual intimacy would soon become an issue. Would Brent pressure her, or let her make the first move? Surely, he had thought about their unspoken feelings toward each other. Part of her wanted to make the leap and the other part held back, afraid of becoming too involved too soon.

Ruthie nudged her leg. She looked to see Penny trying to catch Jasper's tail to no avail. The cat watched Penny, and swished his tail out of her reach. If Clarissa didn't know better, she would swear the cat was teasing the dog on purpose.

"Well, I suppose we should retire for the night. Don't worry, Jasper, boy, I'll set you up with a nice little bed of your own. Daddy will be home the day after tomorrow."

Ruthie led the way with Jasper close behind and the puppy still trying to catch the cat's tail. Clarissa chuckled to herself. What a menagerie.

* * * *

Jimmy arrived early in the morning. "Are ya ready to see if we caught ourselves a rascal?"

"Sure, give me just a minute and I'll be right out." She threw on a jacket and slipped on her tennis shoes. "Okay, let's go."

They arrived at David's place to find the raccoon snarling inside Jimmy's trap. The apple slices had disappeared and the kitchen didn't look much worse than it had when she left last night. Okay, so at least Jimmy had solved the varmint problem. Now she would have to contend with the mess it left behind.

"Thanks, Jimmy. I really appreciate your help. I don't know what I would have done without you."

"No problem, ma'am. You can always count on me. Guess I best be getting 'back. Ellen will have breakfast ready, and she gets mad if I let it get cold." He loaded the trap containing the coon in the back of his truck and got in to leave.

"What will you do with the...the raccoon?" Clarissa looked worried.

"Oh, probably turn him into a coonskin cap. He didn't bite you or Jasper, did he?"

"No, why?" She looked at him with curiosity.

"Because if he bit either of ya, we need to have him tested for rabies." Jimmy frowned with concern.

"No, Jasper stayed outside, and I never got close enough for it to bite me."

A look of relief washed over Jimmy's face as he started up his truck. "Okay, I guess I'll be seeing ya. Call me anytime you need a critter caught." He waved to Clarissa as he drove off and headed down the road.

It saddened Clarissa to know Jimmy would most likely kill the raccoon, but she knew if he didn't it would probably return. She put the thought out of her mind and set her focus on the job at hand. The slow cleaning process started with picking up pots, pans, an empty box of crackers, assorted papers, cans, and packages. Sweeping and mopping the kitchen floor took the longest. Midday came before she had the kitchen back to normal. Clarissa was ready for lunch and a nice relaxing cup of tea.

"Well, Jasper, everything looks normal. I suppose we'd better leave your daddy a note about where to find you when he gets home. He'll probably wonder why I left your pet door closed." She found a pen and piece of paper, scribbled a quick note for David, and left it on the kitchen table where he'd find it.

* * * *

Later, as she was finishing her patient billing accounts for the day, the phone rang.

"Hello?"

"Surprise, it's me," came David's voice through the receiver. "I'll be home a day early. The meetings ended, and I'll arrive first thing tomorrow morning on a plane from Chicago."

"Great, Jasper misses you." Relieved, Clarissa congratulated herself on having dealt with the raccoon incident.

"And what about you?"

"Me?"

"Yeah, are you happy I'm coming home?"

"Uh, yes, of course I am. It will be nice to have my neighbor back and..." Clarissa scrambled for an excuse. "I missed our usual lunch date together."

"Me, too. Well, I'll see you in the morning."

"Oh, David, I forgot to tell you—" Darn, he'd hung up already. Well, he'd find out soon enough about the raccoon incident when he found the note.

Clarissa whistled as she worked. Somehow, David being gone made her feel like her life was incomplete and mundane. He brought sunshine and friendship that made her look forward to Mondays. How strange she should be this happy about him returning when Brent was the man with whom she planned a future. It must be because they were good friends. Why wouldn't she miss a good friend?

* * * *

Knock, knock, knock sounded on the front door of Clarissa's house.

David arrived early, as promised. Clarissa threw on her bathrobe and slippers and ran to answer the door.

"Good morning, pretty lady." He smiled at her as if he wanted to pull her into his arms and kiss her. The scary thing was part of her wanted exactly that. Her stomach felt like she poised on a big hill on a roller coaster ride.

He pulled his hand out from behind his back and handed her a beautiful bouquet of orange, purple, and yellow flowers. "For you. A gift of appreciation for taking such good care of my cat while I was away."

"Oh. They're…they're beautiful." Speechless and breathless all at the same time, Clarissa looked from the flowers to David's smiling face and back to the flowers. "You didn't need to do this. Jasper was no problem." She blushed. Jasper rubbed up against his master with his motor purring at full speed.

"It's nothing really. I picked some wildflowers from my backyard, that's all. And having you watch Jasper was a far better option than having to put him in a kennel."

"I see your point. Thank you, they're lovely." She led David to the kitchen as she prepared to put the flowers in a vase with water. "Would you like to join me for a morning cup of coffee on the porch?"

"Yes, that sounds good."

"I like to sit and watch the birds and breathe in the fresh morning

121

air." She poured two cups of hot coffee and handed one to David. "Cream and sugar?"

"No, this is fine." They headed for the porch followed by all three animals.

"I gather you found my note on your kitchen table." Clarissa sat down on her front porch swing next to David.

"Yes, I did. I assume you had a visitor while I was away?"

"Well, just a pesky raccoon who decided to invite himself into your kitchen and your cabinets. I had to call Jimmy to catch it and then clean up the mess it left behind. That's why Jasper had to stay with me until you came home."

"Interesting, I never thought about a wild animal coming in through Jasper's pet door. The kitchen looks spotless. I guess you must have worked hard. Thank you."

"You're welcome. It wasn't too bad. It could have been worse. There could have been a family of raccoons." Clarissa laughed and David laughed with her.

"Say, how about you let me take you to a country music concert this weekend as sort of a thank you for watching Jasper and cleaning up after that raccoon? George Strait is playing in Columbus Saturday night."

Clarissa thought a minute. Would it be acceptable to go to the concert with her client? She'd done that once, but this was "thank you" for feeding Jasper. How could she turn down George Strait?

"Um...yeah, sure, I guess I could. I love country music." He was her neighbor and her friend. That made it all right, didn't it?

David smiled. "That sounds great. I'll meet you down here at around five p.m. The concert isn't till eight so that'll give us time to get a bite to eat in town first."

"Fine, I look forward to it." Clarissa smiled as she thought about the last concert she attended with David and her jealousy of his former colleague. How silly she was, and why should she be jealous of anyone?

* * * *

The rest of the week flew by and Saturday started out bright with plenty of sunshine. She picked out a simple sunflower-patterned yellow dress and a light green sweater to wear over it. Her reflection in the mirror revealed a schoolgirl of about eighteen. She hoped her youthful look would last her a lifetime. A light spray of perfume and she was ready by the time David arrived.

"I thought we'd have dinner before the concert. Any particular type of restaurant you'd prefer?" David helped Clarissa into his car.

"Well, I am partial to any Oriental food, Chinese or Japanese. What do you like?"

"I haven't been out for Chinese in a while. I miss those little cardboard to-go boxes and fortune cookies."

"Great, take your pick. There are a half a dozen places in any part of town."

"There's one." David pointed to a nearby China Panda across the road in a strip mall.

They entered the restaurant to a serene Chinese setting with giant Oriental fans on the walls and fake bamboo trees in every corner. Black tablecloths and red placemats with Chinese writing covered the tables. A long counter separated the dining area from the kitchen with a lit-up menu board above it. David ordered beef lo-mien with steamed rice and a Pepsi, while Clarissa ordered moo goo gui pan with fried rice and hot tea to drink.

As they ate the excellent food, David filled Clarissa in on his trip. She told him in detail about her raccoon adventure. He laughed when she recounted the part about the raccoon covered in flour.

The concert proved even better than Clarissa had anticipated. She hadn't been to a country music concert in ages and George Strait was one of her favorite male country singers. She hollered and clapped like a schoolgirl, bringing a smile to David's face. He hollered right along with her. By the time intermission arrived, Clarissa, tired but very happy, congratulated herself on agreeing to let David bring her.

When they reached the lobby, Clarissa's eyes grew wide as she saw Brent talking and laughing with a very attractive blonde. Another woman. Who was she, a client or...? Clarissa approached the couple with David by her side.

Chapter Fifteen
~ David to the Rescue ~

"Why Brent, I didn't know you liked George Strait." She smiled at him and waited for his reply.

"Hello, Clarissa." Brent's look of surprise matched his voice. He shot David a sharp look. "This is Trish, one of my clients." Brent smiled, but he ran a finger inside the collar of his shirt. "We ran into each other the other day, and she mentioned this concert. She had tickets and her girlfriend cancelled out on her at the last minute, so she asked if I'd take her. Trish, this is Clarissa Wilford."

"Hi, it's nice to meet you." Trish held out her hand in greeting. "I hope you're enjoying the concert as much as we are."

Clarissa shook hands with Trish, trying to hide her reluctance. "Um, yes, it was great. This is Dr. David Claremont, a neighbor. He's treating me to this concert for looking after his cat while he was out of town."

Clarissa glanced from Brent to David and back to David. Neither one of them looked as uncomfortable as she felt.

"It's nice to meet you, Dr. Claremont. Enjoy the rest of the concert." Trish nodded in farewell as Brent led her back into the concert hall. He had slipped his arm around Trish's back as he guided her.

Clarissa stared after them. *Client, right.* She remained preoccupied for the rest of the concert. Was Trish just a client of Brent's, or was there more to the relationship? Was Brent really the womanizer everyone said he was? No, he must be doing the woman a favor…like he said. After all, it wouldn't do to say no to a client. He didn't act like he was lying during their brief confrontation, but he hurried Trish off.

What had David thought about Brent and what had Brent thought about her and David? She wondered if Brent would suspect her of having an affair with David.

"Is everything ok? I hope you're enjoying the concert." David looked at her with concern.

"Oh, yes. Everything is fine. I'm a bit tired, I suppose." Clarissa touched him gently on the arm to reassure him she was still having a good time.

The long ride home passed in a blur because she dozed off. David seemed to understand it had been a long night and let her sleep. Then the car stopped.

"Wake up, sleepyhead. We're home." David nudged her on the shoulder to wake her as he parked in her driveway.

"We're home already? That was fast."

She looked around and saw her house. She climbed out of the car and walked with David to her door, leaning her head on his shoulder despite her better judgment. He smelled good and was nice and warm in the cool evening air.

"Thank you for the wonderful concert. I really enjoyed it. I guess I'll meet you for lunch Monday at our usual time." She opened the door and entered to avoid an awkward moment in the event David should try to kiss her. She almost felt disappointed when he nodded.

"Thank you for letting me take you. I had a good time too. Sleep well, and I'll see you Monday." David winked at her and waved as he headed back to his car.

* * * *

Sunday afternoon arrived warm and breezy. Ruthie and Penny played in the backyard with Jasper. Off in the distance, a skinny gray dog watched and waited, inching closer every couple of minutes. Clarissa kept a close eye on it, but it wasn't a big dog so she wasn't too worried.

Clarissa worked on her painting of Ruthie and sipped a tall, cold glass of lemonade. A commotion by the fence caught her attention. The dog had worked its way up to the fence, snarled, and snapped at Ruthie and Penny. Ruthie squealed and snorted trying to move away, but her collar was stuck. Penny growled, trying to scare the brute away. Clarissa immediately jumped up and ran for the kitchen, grabbing a pot and pan to bang together.

The noise did nothing to stop the attack by the vicious dog. Jasper took off like an orange rocket, but the dog didn't follow. Clarissa raced inside to grab a broom.

"Shoo, shoo. Get out of here!" she yelled at the snarling animal and poked at it though the fence, but it continued to try to bite at Ruthie.

Loud squeals drowned out the dog noises. Why was the stubborn dog so persistent? It dodged the broom, but kept after Ruthie, snapping and snarling. Clarissa was afraid to try and unhook Ruthie. Those teeth looked lethal.

Bang! A gunshot from behind startled her.

She turned in time to see David running toward the dog with his gun. Frightened by the noise, the gray dog ran as David stopped and fired at it again. The second shot brought it down inches before it reached the woods.

David reached Clarissa as she burst into tears. She cried into his shoulder as he held her close.

"It's okay now. The coyote is dead. He can't hurt you or Ruthie anymore." He patted her on the back reassuring her that the nightmare had ended. "Did Ruthie or Penny get bitten?"

"I...I don't think so." She stooped to inspect her animals, but found no bite marks.

"Just the same, I'd better take the coyote in for rabies testing to be sure. We don't want to take any chances."

"Coyote? I thought it was a feral dog." She stared at him, eyes wide.

"No, that was a coyote. Didn't you recognize the gray fur, the pointed muzzle and ears?"

"I thought it was someone's stray dog or something. We've had feral dogs before, and I always called the animal control officer. I am so glad you came. I didn't know what to do. It wouldn't leave." She sniffled back a sob as she regained control of her senses.

"Thank Jasper. He came tearing in through the open door and jumped on me with his claws. Then he took off back through the door again wanting me to follow. Instinct made me grab my gun. I knew something was wrong the minute I stepped outside and heard Ruthie squealing. Pigs make a lot noise when threatened."

"Why did this happen? I've never seen a coyote this close before and so persistent." She frowned at the disturbing thought.

"It must have been hungry. It probably had already killed or scared off much of the wildlife in the woods. Guess he saw your Ruthie and thought she would make a perfect meal."

David picked up the coyote's body and lugged it to the bed of his truck. Once he stowed it, he turned to Clarissa. "I'll get back to you with the test results when I find out. If it had rabies, you'll want to get Ruthie and Penny tested at your vet."

"Yes, thank you, David. I don't know what I would have done if you weren't here." She shuddered at the thought, wrapping her sweater tighter around herself.

"No problem. What are neighbors for if they can't help out?" He grinned at her and left.

* * * *

By the time she arrived at the Café Corner Monday to meet David for lunch, Clarissa had reached a high level of anxiety. She worried whether or not the coyote David shot had rabies and she could hardly focus on anything else.

"No worries." David smiled as he approached her. "The coyote didn't have rabies, just a rotten case of bad breath." Laughing, he took a seat across from her at their usual booth.

"That's not even funny." She frowned at him and smacked him on the arm.

"Ouch." He rubbed his arm as if it hurt, grinning at her like a kid caught robbing the cookie jar. "I'm sorry. I was just trying to make you feel better. I know how shook up you were over the whole incident."

"I appreciate it. I was thinking I should get an electric fence."

"That's not a bad idea. Jimmy and I could probably install it for you."

"Thanks, great idea. I'd really be grateful."

"Sure, no problem. Just let me know when you need it done, and I'll get together with Jimmy."

"I guess it's a good thing you had that gun. I never thought I'd be happy to see anyone with a gun until that coyote tried to get my Ruthie."

"Guns have their place and come in handy sometimes. Can't imagine if I didn't have one."

David was a good neighbor. He might be right about guns, but she still didn't like them.

"I wanted to thank you again for the concert Saturday night. I enjoyed it."

Embarrassed, she glanced down at the table. He made her feel like a giddy.

"It was my pleasure. I had fun, too, and you deserved it after having to clean up my kitchen from the raccoon mess." His eyes sparkled with laughter.

By the time they finished their lunch, Clarissa was ready to get back to work. She bid David good-bye and headed off to run a couple of errands and do a bit of shopping. Soon, she returned home to do her medical billing work.

* * * *

In her home office, the paperwork had piled up. Sighing, she attacked the mess. The phone rang when she was halfway through the current stack. She smiled as she recognized Brent's number on the caller ID.

"Hello, Brent, what's up?"

She waited, curious to hear what he'd say. They hadn't spoken since the concert, and she wasn't sure how he'd felt about seeing her with David there.

"No much. Just wondering how you feel about that fishing date?"

She raised her right eyebrow. "Um...it's ok. I can't say I'm very good at it though. Why?"

"Well," he began slowly. "I thought we might go on a picnic fishing outing this weekend at Lake Logan. That is, if you're interested."

"Sure, I am. You may have to help me with the fishing part though. I haven't done much fishing in a long time. I'm such a klutz, but I can make a great picnic lunch."

"I'll pick you and your picnic lunch up Sunday at your place around ten, okay?"

"Sure, I'll see you then."

Relief struck as she hung up the phone. The woman he was with at the concert must have just been a client or a friend. How else could he act like everything was fine? This time she'd give him the benefit of the doubt. The rest of the week Clarissa floated on air. She could hardly wait to see Brent .The picnic sounded like fun. It would be perfect.

She'd make him a mouthwatering lunch and wear an outfit to make him drool. She wanted everything to be perfect. If he had intentions, it would be time for him to make a move. She could picture it so clearly in her mind, a romantic outing followed by an evening at home—his hands and lips all over hers and the heat searing through her and consuming both of them.

She was tired of being alone. Her pets were great company, but she longed for intimacy and passion with a man.

Whoa! Her imagination was running wild. That was all fine when it was Brent, but too often her thoughts ended up with David. When they did, shame engulfed her. Brent was a great catch, so why did part of her want someone else, someone so unsuitable?

Setting aside her disturbing thoughts, Clarissa focused on her billing.

The week went faster than she'd expected. The Logan Antique Mall was now bringing in a nice profit for her, despite the gloomy economy. She never did find out who bought her expensive piece, but she still suspected David.

When she walked her pets Friday afternoon, she noticed the orange flags had disappeared. She had seen no sign of digging along the road and no crews of workmen. Friday night she slept well and woke with a vague memory of a wedding, but as the groom turned toward her the alarm went off. Why would she dream about a wedding? Maybe the coming date with Brent triggered it. Sometimes she had silly dreams.

Chapter Sixteen
~ The Not-so-Perfect Picnic ~

The morning of the picnic with Brent had arrived. Clarissa wanted everything to be perfect. No way did she want Brent to think her overdone. Lord knows Donna had that department covered.

She hurried through her morning chores, cleaned up the breakfast dishes, and took Ruthie and Penny for a quick walk. When they reached David's, she saw no sign of him this morning. As she walked, she mulled over what to wear for a picnic. No skirt. Slacks? The weather forecast called for hot and sunny. Shorts?

Once home, she settled on knee-length brown shorts and a tan, pullover blouse. Pulling her hair into a ponytail, she applied her makeup. She wanted a natural appearance, but she wanted to look her best.

Next, she packed the picnic basket with fried chicken, baked beans, and potato salad. She placed the apple pie on top. Finished, she reviewed her mental list, but couldn't think of anything else. She tossed in a bottle of water and considered tea or lemonade, but decided to wait and ask Brent.

When he arrived, he held out a bottle of blackberry wine.

"My favorite." Clarissa grinned at him. "It'll go well with the apple pie." She added two wine glasses to the basket.

"Sounds good." Brent licked his lips in anticipation. He moved closer to her and put his hand on her shoulder.

"Ouch." He jumped back and rubbed his calf. "What the..."

Clarissa looked down to see what happened. "Are you okay?"

"Uh, yeah, but that pig bit me." He pointed at Ruthie.

"Ruthie?"

Clarissa stared down at her pig and glanced at Penny next to her. Ruthie looked the picture of innocence. Next to her, Penny wagged her tail.

"I'm sorry. Are you sure Ruthie bit you? She's never done anything like that."

"Of course I'm sure," he snapped. A hint of anger colored Brent's voice. He looked from the pig to Clarissa. He seemed to sense her dismay.

"It's okay. Maybe she thought I planned to attack you. Someone told me you had a pig, but I never knew pigs bit people."

"Ruthie's never bitten anyone." Clarissa frowned in frustration, uncertain what to think.

Brent grinned and held out his hand. "It's okay, no harm done. Shall we?"

"If you're sure. Ruthie, what's gotten into you?"

She stared down at Ruthie's upturned face, puzzled. Ruthie looked as if nothing had happened, her ears perked and her eyes bright and shiny. Clarissa had no idea what to say or do.

"I'm so sorry."

"Forget it. Let's get this show on the road." Brent headed for the door with the picnic basket in hand. He appeared to dismiss the incident as unimportant.

"Be good, Ruthie, Penny. Mommy will be back soon." She patted Ruthie gently on her side, still confused over the incident, and rubbed Penny's soft ears before following Brent out the front door.

Why had Ruthie nipped at Brent, if she had a sweet temperament and even David with his gun hadn't bothered her? Ruthie always shied away from strange newcomers like Jasper, but she had never ever nipped even the cat or Penny.

"I've decided we'll go to Leonard's Lake. It has fewer people than Logan and doesn't allow powerboats and Jet Skis."

"I've never been there," Clarissa said. "It sounds nice. I'd love to not have to deal with those noisy outboard motors."

They arrived at the small private lake around noon and saw only a few other cars parked in the lot. Brent carried the basket and blanket toward the water. He selected a grassy spot near a large maple by the edge of the water. Clarissa spread out the big beach blanket and put out plates and silverware while Brent filled two wine glasses half full with wine. A pair of mallard ducks floated nearby trailed by baby ducklings, and the sun shone overhead. A gentle breeze swayed the trees, and the smell of fresh grass filled the air. A perfect day for a picnic.

"Shall we?" Brent motioned toward the bountiful spread of food before them.

"Sure." Clarissa raised her glass of wine and touched it to his.

"A toast to our first picnic together.—the first of many." He gazed into Clarissa's eyes and held her mesmerized.

She stared back. The intensity of his gaze sent shivers along her spine. She almost wished they had gone to Lake Logan. This area had few people. While she wanted to see where the relationship could go, she didn't like the idea of Brent ravishing her on the grass. Titillating, but she wasn't sure she liked the idea of that happening with other people around. Excessive public displays of passionate affection still made her squirm.

"Cheers."

Clarissa blinked, uncertain what to do or say. She hoped Brent couldn't see through her to those wicked thoughts.

"When I was a boy, my dad used to take me fishing. I guess that's why I love it now."

Clarissa could almost see a miniature Brent trailing behind his father. The image made her smile. When he said nothing more, she sought to fill the almost awkward silence before any thoughts of lovemaking could pop into her head.

"My dad didn't do much fishing, but he worked hard to support the family," Clarissa said. "I have a brother, but Dad never spent much time with us except on vacations. I've always envied large families and want one. Five kids sounds perfect."

"Whoa, that would mean a lot of work, and your job would suffer." Brent looked uncomfortable with the idea of a large family.

"I work at home, but that might be so. I hadn't thought about it that way."

Brent smiled with narrowed eyes as if they played some sort of truth or dare game. "Any skeletons in your closet?"

"Once I dated a guy from Lancaster, but he proved to be a jerk and a womanizer." Clarissa frowned as she remembered her ex-boyfriend Tony.

"That's too bad." Brent looked sympathetic and reddened slightly as he looked at the food.

He reached for her hand, kissed her palm, and sent shivers up her arm. "You don't have anything to worry about with me, babe. I'm loyal to the woman I choose. Even when my ex-wife cheated on me with my ex-best friend, I never cheated on her."

Overwhelming sympathy for Brent washed over Clarissa as she thought how awful it must have been for him to be betrayed not only by his wife, but his best friend. It was something they shared.

He leaned toward her and pulled her into his arms. Lowering his mouth to hers, he kissed her. Heat enveloped her, rushing through her veins, and she leaned into him. Brent pulled her close to his broad chest, and she melted against him.

A few intense minutes of breathless kisses left her gasping. "That was something else."

He smiled with a raised eyebrow. "You think so? I have plenty more where that came from for later." Winking at her, he waited for her response.

Anxious to move things to a safer footing, she pondered how to ask him about the rumors Geneva and David had mentioned. "I heard a few…uh…things about your business."

"Good, I hope." Brent looked at her and waited.

"Well…" She hesitated, wanting to find the best way to ask him about the nasty rumors without insulting him or making him defensive. She deliberated for a moment.

"Donna Gilead spoke highly of you. Is she a client?"

Brent grinned. "The Logan real estate lady? No, but now that you mention it, maybe I should contact her."

"I also…um heard some of your elderly clients lost money."

"Where did you hear that?" He frowned and looked intimidating.

She'd annoyed him, she just knew it. "Um, well townsfolk talk, you know." Clarissa tried to suppress the uneasiness from her voice.

"Any type of investment is a risk. You win some, you lose some.

Not every company performs as well as you hope, especially now." His voice remained calm and steady. "No one can predict the market with any certainty."

"I know that, but some of the elderly count on investments for income or retirement. Any losses hurt them."

None of the ones she had met wanted anything but secure bonds and CDs. Most would hate any sort of risk. Small merchants and farmers scrimped and worked too hard for their money to tolerate losses.

"Hey, I lose, too. The fees they pay barely cover the costs. Those who can't afford it shouldn't invest. Besides, I know plenty of elderly who squander their money gambling in casinos. Investing money is a much better use of it."

"Maybe you should advise them to buy CDs," Clarissa suggested.

"They don't pay anything these days. The only way to make money is to invest. The riskier the investment, the more gain. How about some of that delicious-looking apple pie?" Brent stared at the dessert and grinned.

"Ah, yeah," Clarissa said and cut him a piece.

Yeah, right. Didn't Brent understand these folks? With that kind of philosophy, she wouldn't want him handling her money. Did he feel the same way about his personal relationships? What kind of a lifelong partner would that make him? He must not know these people well or just not care. If he had, he wouldn't have suggested investments with any significant risk.

He smiled at her as he put down his plate. "You make a great apple pie."

She shouldn't rush to judge him. People who jumped to conclusions annoyed her, and she had always vowed not to do that.

Finished with dessert, Brent removed the fishing gear from the trunk of his car and set it by the shore. They cleaned up their picnic area, packed everything away, and loaded it in the car. At the dock, Brent rented a small boat for two. He held the craft steady for Clarissa and seated her in the stern. Taking the oars, he rowed them toward the middle of the lake to fish for what he referred to as a monster catch.

"I hope they're biting today." Brent rigged up his line with a lure and cast. "The trick is to aim toward the shore when you're in a boat and toward the middle of the lake when you're fishing from the shoreline. Here, let me show you how to cast." He placed his warm hands around hers, sending tingles along her arms.

Clarissa knew the basics of fishing, but decided to play along with Brent. Men loved to feel in charge. After he demonstrated how to cast her line, Clarissa tried, but caught him on the back of his shirt.

"Ouch!" He pulled his shirt off to remove the hook. His broad chest made her want to touch him.

"I'm so sorry. Let me see your back. I hope I didn't hurt you."

Brent looked irritated. "No, I'm fine. It happens with beginners sometimes. Next time try to cast it farther out."

After a couple more tries, she felt her confidence rise. The line landed in the water and not on Brent. After several more tries, she even managed to catch a small bluegill.

"Look at that, you caught one." Brent beamed at her. "It's too small to keep. Here, I'll throw it back."

He appeared to think his teaching had accomplished it. She suppressed a grin. Her father had taken her fishing a few times, but it had been years ago. Tony, too, had taken her fishing. With deft fingers, Brent detached the hook and tossed the fish into the water. To Clarissa's relief, it swam off.

"We make a good team. You live so far out though, you could consider living in Athens."

His words took her by surprise and made her catch her breath. "I'm…I'm a country girl."

"Athens has a lot to offer."

"Yeah, rowdy students. The beer busts are something else. All that noise and crowds of people. I'd much rather have a nice dinner in town and then come home to the peace and quiet of the country."

"If you sell your land, you could make a bundle. I hear some big conglomerate wants a place around Logan. You could buy or rent in Athens or…"

"Or?"

"I have plenty of room. We could share expenses, and I can help you with investing the money from selling your place."

He hadn't mentioned marriage or love. "Uh, we've only had a few dates. Isn't it a bit soon to talk about sharing quarters?"

"There are compensations." He looked at her with a crooked smile. "You'll love the city and the people."

Mulling over his words and what he meant, she prepared to cast again. Then, she glanced down to the bottom of the boat. Shocked, she stared at a granddaddy-long-legs crawling near her foot. A spider! A nasty, big spider. She hated them.

"Ahhh!" she screamed, leaping away. She jumped on the stern seat, and the boat wobbled. It tipped first right and then left.

"What the hell?" Brent stared at her. "Clarissa, sit down or—"

Clarissa shifted from foot to foot staring at the spider. She threw the rod at it. The horrible thing scuttled toward her.

"No! Get away!"

Brent half-rose from his seat and leaned toward her. "Sit down, or you'll end up in the water."

"Kill it, kill it!" she yelled. The long, spindly legs moved the bulbous brown body toward her.

"Kill what?"

"That…that spider, that's what."

Frightened and anxious to avoid the creature, she tried to move back, but there was nowhere to go. Struggling to keep her balance, she leaned to the side instead. The boat tilted the same way. Like a tipsy windmill, she waved her arms in the air. She couldn't catch her balance.

Flailing, she fell. She cried out as the cold water surrounded her.

Chapter Seventeen
~ Sink or Swim ~

The boat tipped and dumped Clarissa and Brent into the water. Poles and the tackle box tagged along. The poles, weighed down by the reels, sank, but the yellow tackle box bobbed up and down.

Clarissa treaded water and stared in horror at the upside-down boat. All because of a spider. After splashing about for a moment, Brent managed to turn the boat over and grabbed the tackle box. He climbed back into the boat.

"Here, take my arm." He reached out to Clarissa and helped her scramble into the boat. "Why on earth did you stand up?" He looked furious.

"I hate spiders, always have." She shuddered and rubbed her arms, glad to see no sign of a bite or the horrible spider.

"A spider wouldn't hurt you."

"I know, but…"

Men never understood women's reactions to insects. The look on his face said it all—'leave it to a silly woman'. It would have been worse if neither of them could swim or the weather was cold.

Two soaked people dripped water in the boat. Staring down at her own bedraggled state and Brent's, Clarissa burst out laughing.

"What's so funny? I bought that reel at the bait and tackle store just last week. It wasn't cheap. Now it's history." His face turned a sullen red. "Of all the stupid…" He stopped before saying anything more.

Still laughing, she struggled to apologize. "I'm so sorry. I don't know why I'm laughing. I guess so I don't cry." She managed to suppress more giggles. Why couldn't he see the humor in the situation?

He rowed in silence to the shore. Brent avoided looking at her as they tied the boat to the dock. She hoped he wouldn't hold a grudge against her. Clarissa wondered if he was going to speak or just fume.

"I'm really very sorry. I didn't tip the boat on purpose, but I can't stand spiders. I hate the ugly things. I have this thing about them since I was a little girl."

Brent sighed. "Women and bugs. It's okay. I know you didn't mean to dump us into the lake." He looked a little less irritated and covered her hand with his. He gave her a reassuring squeeze. "Why don't we go to your place and shed these wet clothes?"

"Right." She smiled at him, relieved he didn't appear angry.

They packed up everything and drove toward her place as she tried hard to suppress another fit of laughter. The vision of the two of them dripping wet wouldn't leave her mind.

"You know, you really should consider moving in with me," Brent said. "Besides, an investment company, Trade Industries, is looking for property in your area. I hear they pay well." He looked at her, waiting for a response.

"Really, that's interesting. They came up on my caller ID a couple weeks ago. I thought they were telemarketers." Clarissa shifted in her seat.

This conversation made her uncomfortable. She liked the country and had no desire to sell. Why should he urge her that way? Okay, so he said they could live together, but what exactly did he want from her?

"No, they were out here not long ago surveying the land for possible development for a housing community. You could profit quite nicely if you sold your land to them." He was looking at her like a hungry wolf about to eat an exhausted deer.

"No, I'd never sell my place. I love my little piece of heaven. It's tranquil and not crowded. Not to mention the gorgeous view of the tree-covered hills. No, I would never give up my dream home. Besides, Ruthie and Penny would never forgive me, and I would never forgive myself either." She frowned as they pulled into her driveway.

"I understand, but the city has advantages, too. Career opportunities, more clients, people to socialize with, and lights everywhere at night."

"Ah, but my quiet time is better than an office job, and too many people annoy me. When it gets dark in the country, you can see a sky full of stars. It's the most beautiful sight I've ever seen."

Brent said nothing. When they reached her driveway, he parked in front of the porch. To Clarissa's relief, their wet clothes had begun to dry. Brent stepped out of the car and came round to open the door for her. He held her hand in his as they walked up the pathway to the front door. His warm, confident clasp reassured her.

"You have a beautiful place." Brent gazed at the scenery. "How long have you lived here?"

"Oh, two, almost three years now. It's the kind of place I always dreamed of when I was growing up…that and a family of my own." She blushed and looked down at her feet.

"I see." He smiled at her as if he understood and could see himself as that family man.

Ruthie greeted Clarissa and Brent at the door as they entered. She reached down to pat Ruthie on the back and Penny on the head.

"Hi, babies, Mommy missed you."

Still soggy from her swim, she turned to Brent. "Why don't you go in the bathroom and get out of your wet clothes. Put on the robe hanging on the door, and I'll throw your clothes in the dryer."

Clarissa pointed him toward the bathroom and then went to her room to change. She slid on a pair of jeans and a red, short-sleeved sweater. The jeans hugged her body and accentuated her waist. She repaired her makeup in her dresser mirror and sprayed on some lilac body spray. A comb helped settle down her hair.

When she returned to the living room, Brent lolled on the couch. Ruthie sulked in the corner while Penny sat nearby wagging her tail and waiting for attention. Ruthie's behavior puzzled Clarissa. It almost appeared as if she disliked Brent. He looked comical wearing her bathrobe, but sexy at the same time, with a fringe of dark chest hair showing and lots of leg. Maybe Ruthie didn't like him in one of Clarissa's garments.

Anxious to smooth things over, she wondered if something to drink and nibble on might help. "I'll bring us some refreshments from the kitchen. Would you like tea or coffee?"

"A good, hot cup of tea sounds perfect." Brent smiled at her with his dazzling, sexy smile and a 'come here, babe' look.

"I'll toss your clothes in the dryer and get the tea. Be back in a few minutes."

She headed for the kitchen. After putting Brent's clothes in the drier, she opened the cupboard. Selecting the powdered green tea, the kind her mother always used, she added an assortment of fancy Pepperidge Farm cookies she kept as a special treat to serve with it.

The sound of romantic music floated from the living room. Brent must have found some CDs to play. Images of the two of them making love in her queen-sized bed ignited a fire in her blood. She wondered if he was as good in bed as he looked like he'd be. She envisioned him as the kind of man who would take control, but be gentle at the same time. He really had a way with women from what Donna, the real estate lady, had implied about his reputation. Could she trust him to be faithful to one woman, or would he be like her ex-boyfriend Tony and move on to someone else when he tired of her? If so, where would that leave her?

Pushing such thoughts aside, Clarissa filled a kettle with water and put it on the stove to boil, then busied herself with organizing the tea things. Uncertain how he liked his tea, she poured milk into a cream pitcher and set it with the sugar bowl on a large wooden serving tray, with a couple slices of fresh lemon. To her, green tea required nothing.

Her favorite Japanese teapot and cup set with cherry blossom designs added a festive air. The assortment of Pepperidge Farm cookies on a matching serving plate completed the set. With some cherry blossom paper napkins and little teaspoons to stir the tea, she stood back to examine the tray with a critical eye. She wanted to impress Brent and make him forget his unplanned bath in the lake.

The kettle whistled, signaling the boiling water. She turned off the stove and filled the teapot. "That ought to do it."

When she entered the living room, she glimpsed Ruthie still in the corner and could almost swear the little pig scowled at Brent. Penny tugged at Brent's robe, and he pushed her away until she finally lay at his feet still hoping for some attention. Ruthie was friendly with almost everyone. Clarissa decided Ruthie was jealous of Brent. Poor Penny just looked up at him with her sad eyes, but he ignored her. She hadn't brought any men here since Tony.

"Come sit by me." Brent patted the cushion next to him on the couch. He leaned against the back of the sofa, and the robe gaped, exposing his chest and his muscular legs.

If only he knew the effect, he had on her…or maybe he did. Clarissa set the tray down on the coffee table and proceeded to serve the tea. Her hands shook as she struggled to steady her nerves. She sat down, poured them each a cup of tea, and offered Brent the cookies. He took the tea and a shortbread cookie with a raspberry center.

To calm herself, she asked him about his work. "Tell me more about what you do. I've never really thought about investing before. How do you advise people about specific investments and any risks?"

His earlier responses to her questions had left her unsatisfied. She wanted, in a tactful way, to have a better explanation than "sometimes you win and sometimes you lose." She wanted him to show the same spirit of caring and concern for his clients as he showed for her.

He happily changed the subject, enthusiasm lighting his features. His eyes sparkled. "I start by sitting down with my clients, reviewing their current finances, and then help them structure their budget to free funds for potential investments.

"Next, I establish a portfolio for them based on their choices of investments and advise them of the best moneymakers at the lowest risk possible. Of course, there's always some risk, as I said before. Finally, I have them fill out an automatic withdrawal from their bank account each month to transfer the investment funds into their stock account. I take a small percentage of their profits, but with a number of clients it provides a comfortable living, enough to support me and a family." He grinned at her.

Nothing there to cause any problems, but that automatic withdrawal could create difficulty for some. "So what happens if your clients lose money?"

"Most of the time they gain, and, when stocks falls, they only have to wait a while. If the client takes my advice and stays in the market, the stocks will rise again. However, sometimes a client elects to withdraw from the falling market and then they lose."

"I guess if you were in it for the long haul, you're better off to stick it out," Clarissa mused.

"Exactly, I'm glad you see the advantages of that. I can do a lot for you, if you'd let me." His face promised all sorts of things, and Clarissa's temperature rose.

Perhaps he sensed her reluctance. "We'll talk about your investment program later. For now, let's concentrate on us."

He eased his arm around her, and his nearness intensified that fiery sensation, but also sent chills through her at the same time. He drew her close against his firm chest. A trace of cologne not washed away by the lake water tickled her nose and led her to wonder how the hair on his chest would feel against her bare skin. He leaned closer.

Just then, something solid landed on Clarissa. She looked down to see Ruthie sprawled in her lap. She laughed at the sight and rubbed gently behind the pig's soft ears.

"What is it, sweetie? Are you jealous?" She cuddled Ruthie for a moment and kissed the top of her nose before setting her down on the floor. "It's okay, baby, you can relax, Ruthie."

"You kiss your pig?" Brent looked disgusted. "Pigs have germs."

"Pigs have no more germs than humans. Despite what people think, pigs are clean animals. At least my Ruthie is. I bathe her and groom her daily." Brent's attitude annoyed her, but then he knew nothing about pigs and especially not about Ruthie.

Struggling to smooth things over, she remembered his family. "You said you have a daughter. You must miss her."

Clarissa wanted to learn about Brent's former life and what kind of husband and father he had been. It might tell her if he was marriage material.

He snorted. "No, not really. She's a little bitch just like her mother...all about money and power."

Blinking, she pulled away to stare at him, shocked. How could he call his own daughter that...word? What kind of a monster felt that way about his child? No way could she believe he really meant that about his daughter. Surely, he had some reason for his view.

"Why...why do you say that?"

"Because it's true. Sarah took me for everything I had and child support. She told me she deserved it for being married to me. She called me a first-class pig." At the look on Clarissa's face, he stopped. "I mean…well, she did say pig, 'a male chauvinist pig,' but you've heard that before I'm sure, no offense to Ruthie."

"Yes, I've heard it." Clarissa sighed. "Did your daughter have a pet? Did you ever own a dog or a cat?"

"We had a cat once, but it clawed up my good boots so I took it down the road and dumped it."

"What?" Clarissa frowned in astonishment. "The poor animal. How could you do that to a defenseless creature?"

"It wasn't defenseless—not with those claws. Besides, someone probably took it in, so I'm sure it wasn't homeless for long." Brent waved it off as if it was no big deal.

Clarissa edged away, uncertain she wanted any more of this. Uneasiness consumed her.

As if sensing her confusion, Brent slid closer. His mobile mouth approached hers. His warm breath almost tickled her. His lips covered hers, and he nibbled with surprising gentleness. Little by little, he increased the pressure against her mouth and licked her lips. He tasted of green tea and raspberries.

Taken by surprise, she responded at once and melted into his embrace. He slipped nimble fingers under her sweater. His hands on her skin sent desire through her limbs. He pressed her back on the couch. Heat consumed Clarissa. No way did she want him to stop.

A horrific squeal rent the air and nearly burst Clarissa's eardrum. A hard nose bumped her arm. She looked down to see Ruthie trying to climb on the sofa.

"Ruthie, what's the matter with you?" Clarissa set her on the floor and turned to Brent. "I'm so sorry. I don't know why she's acting this way."

Irritation flushed Brent's face, but he planted his lips on hers with determination. His fingers unfastened button after button on her jeans with one hand. He pushed up her sweater and tugged at her jeans. Fire suffused Clarissa. She closed her eyes.

"Yewoouch!"

Her eyes snapped open. Ruthie clung to Brent's ankle. Her little teeth gave her purchase, and she hung on like a cocklebur. Penny lay to one side chewing on Brent's shoes.

Brent tried to shake Ruthie off and pushed with his other foot to dislodge her, but she hung on and refused to let him loose.

Concerned, Clarissa feared for Ruthie. "Don't kick her, you might hurt her."

She pulled her sweater down and picked up Ruthie. She held the trembling body close and crooned to the little pig.

"Are you okay, baby?"

"What about me?" Brent rubbed his ankle and examined it to see if Ruthie's teeth had pierced the skin.

Brent. Had Ruthie hurt him? Clarissa stared at his ankle. No blood flowed and no broken skin. "It's a tiny red mark, it'll fade in no time." She looked at Ruthie, perplexed by the pig's strange behavior.

Eyes wide, Brent starred at Clarissa in disbelief. "You prefer a pig to me?"

Chapter Eighteen
~ Scratch One Man ~

Anger flashed across Brent's face. "I'm better than a pig or any other pet for that matter." He scowled at Ruthie and then Penny.

"Hey, leave my shoe alone." In a huff, Brent snatched it away from Penny, who dodged him as he took a swipe at her with his shoe.

"Stop it!" Clarissa shouted and set Ruthie down to scramble to her feet. "Either you accept my pets and learn to get along with them, or we don't have a future together."

"They need to learn their place and to get along with *me*. You spoil them," he accused, pointing his finger at her. "A little discipline would do wonders."

"Let's just call it a day." She left him sitting on the couch in the living room and marched off to retrieve his clothes from the dryer. When she returned, Brent was on his feet.

She shoved the bundle at him. "Here are your clothes."

"You want me to leave?" He looked stunned. A stare of incredulous shock crossed his face.

"Yes, you'd best leave, now."

He snatched the clothes from her with a glare and stalked toward the bathroom.

Clarissa cuddled Ruthie close while she waited for Brent to return. With Ruthie soothed, she put her down next to Penny, gathered the dishes, and took the serving tray into the kitchen. Ruthie and Penny trotted close on her heels as if seeking protection. She placed a carrot in Ruthie's bowl and a dog treat in Penny's.

A door slammed in the living room. Clarissa hurried to the window to see Brent's car take off in a spray of gravel and a swirl of dust down the driveway.

"Well, scratch one man." She sighed.

She stared down at Ruthie and Penny who looked at her with bright eyes. "Maybe you two know more about men than I do. My head didn't like what he said, but he sure knew how to turn me on." She sighed again. "Thanks for saving me from a colossal mistake."

She smiled down at the two. Ruthie wagged her tail, and Penny jumped up and down.

"What do you say we take a walk and get some fresh air?" She took Ruthie's harness and lead from the hook by the door as Ruthie and Penny pranced about her ankles, anxious to go.

Clarissa hooked up Ruthie's harness, and the three of them headed out the door.

The evening sun hung low in the sky, and the colors on the horizon astounded Clarissa. Too bad Brent wasn't the man she wanted him to be. Why did she always manage to pick guys that appeared so perfect in the beginning and ended up being such jerks in the end? Good looks and sex appeal never made up for a lack of understanding and real concern for others. Would she ever find the man of her dreams and have the family she'd always wanted?

Jasper jumped out of the bushes the way he always did to join them on their walk. She, Ruthie, and Penny had grown used to this by now so it no longer came as a surprise as it had the first time he scared them half to death. Ruthie no longer acted frightened or resentful towards Jasper, but still gave him wide berth in spite of her acceptance.

"Hi there, Jasper. What are you up to this evening? Out hunting mice and other rodents in the fields I suppose." Clarissa stoked Jasper, relishing his soft, silky fur.

Such a large, handsome, orange cat. David must feed Jasper well. She had always liked cats and had one as a child, until one day it ran off. She supposed a stranger took it in…at least she hoped so. Sometimes, when she saw dead cats on the road, she wondered if the same fate had befallen her beloved Sassy.

Clarissa ambled along with Ruthie and Penny while Jasper padded beside them. Her thoughts returned to Brent. Imagine the nerve of that man! How could he expect her to overlook his attitude to his daughter and his treatment of her own pets? Her ignorance and his sexiness had prevented her from seeing him as a complete jerk. As she walked, Clarissa realized she'd blinded herself to his faults.

"You tried to tell me, girls, didn't you? I let my physical senses stifle my reason." She reached down to rub Ruthie on top of her nose, one of the softest parts of a pig, and patted Penny's side.

"Let's go home, girls. I'll fix us a special dinner, and we'll watch a movie together. I'll even fix you your favorite bedtime treat—popcorn."

* * * *

Clarissa stopped in at the doctor's office on Monday for her weekly exchange of paperwork and client files. At least work provided plenty of distraction from the sorry state of her love life.

Geneva, the receptionist, looked up as she entered and smiled at her. "How are things going with Brent?"

"They're not." Clarissa frowned, debating what to say. She plopped down in the chair next to Geneva's desk.

The receptionist looked concerned. "What happened? I thought you two were headed toward wedded bliss."

"Turns out he's another complete jerk."

"How so?"

"He…has no sense of humor, and…he.,.he kicked at Ruthie and Penny. Why would anyone kick a defenseless animal?" Clarissa appealed to Geneva. "Well, maybe not totally defenseless. Ruthie nipped at him, and Penny chewed his fancy shoes."

"He kicked Ruthie and Penny? The brute!"

"Yeah. I don't think they liked him."

"I don't either. Serves him right. Ruthie and Penny have good judgment."

"I guess. That's one man gone and none waiting in the wings." Clarissa sighed.

Geneva looked at her with sympathy. "Don't worry, dear, your perfect mate is out there."

"I know, but I really thought he was the one. Why can't I find Mr. Right?"

"Perhaps your ideal man isn't as far away as you think." Geneva grinned as if she knew something Clarissa didn't.

"Yeah, perhaps you're right. I just need to stop trying too hard I guess."

"That's right. Let love find you, dear, not the other way around."

The morning flew by and before she realized it, lunchtime arrived. Clarissa headed to Café Corner. David already sat at their favorite booth waiting for her. When she approached him, he looked up at her with a broad smile and waved. She realized she enjoyed spending time with him because he always made her feel appreciated and interesting. He didn't even mind her clumsiness.

"Hello, Sunshine," he called out to her as she approached.

"Hi." She blushed and took a seat across from him.

"What's the news?" David looked at her with his big blue eyes. They always made her weak in the knees.

"Not much." She didn't want him to know about Brent, at least not yet.

"Would you like to hear my latest theory?"

"Sure." Her curiosity roused, she waited on his response.

"I think your coyote came from the city. I've heard there were some packs just outside of Lancaster that have migrated toward Logan since they started the bypass. Apparently, the construction destroyed some of their homes, and they had to find new ones. Many settled around the outskirts of Logan. They're territorial. I think the one I shot at your place had been displaced and was looking to establish his new territory on your land."

Clarissa's eyes widened in realization. "That would make sense. He must have figured Ruthie was food."

"Yep. So, we should keep a close eye out in case any more show up. I thought I'd get Jimmy to help put up that electric fence for you, if that's okay with you."

"Sure, that would be great. You can do it this Saturday if it's convenient for you."

"Saturday it is then. I'll get with Jimmy and let you know if there's any problem. If you don't hear from me, you can assume we'll be there at ten Saturday morning."

"Sounds good." Clarissa smiled.

They talked about a number of things that day, everything except for Brent. Either David knew and said nothing out of respect, or he hadn't heard the news. Somehow, she figured he knew and refrained from raising the subject. Brent would blow over like other failed relationships and leave another hole in her heart. She needed to stay busy and focus on the positive. She thanked the powers-that-be that she found out before it was too late. What a nightmare it would have been if she had married him. The ex-wife should have been a clue.

* * * *

Several days had passed since the breakup, and life was returning to normal. One afternoon, Clarissa stopped by her mailbox and found a note. When she opened it, it read, *"Watch your back, bitch!"* The note consisted of pasted newspaper clippings to make a message. No handwriting gave away the perpetrator's identity.

Who wanted to frighten her? She had no enemies. Brent was too sensible to do something like this. Besides, he could have any woman he wanted, any woman but her. She'd stop by the sheriff's office later and file a report just to be safe. How dare someone harass her like this? She did nothing to deserve it. She would see to it the person behind the note was caught and prosecuted.

The next day, a disturbing phone call came. She heard only heavy breathing on the other end followed by a disconnect. Caller ID offered no number. Who had called and why? The news carried stories about stalkers and serial killers, but she had no enemies. She called the phone company and they suggested she get, even though she had caller ID, phone-tracking equipment from her local electronics store to trace the calls. Cell phones, however, made it wasted effort, but who knew. Some people weren't very smart. She planned to pick up the equipment that afternoon.

The police agreed they would check the note for fingerprints, but if the person took enough care to cut and paste the words instead of handwriting the note, they probably wore gloves to avoid leaving fingerprints. Stamps came on ready-to-peel paper strips and a self-sealing envelope had been used. That eliminated trace DNA left behind.

Somebody knew police procedures, watched those forensic shows, or was just too smart to leave clues. As she got ready to leave for the phone company office, her brother Cliff called.

"Hi, Sis. What's up?"

"Not much, I have to run an errand in town. What's up with you and Mieko?" She decided not to mention the note or phone call yet. She didn't want to worry him.

"Well, we were thinking about stopping by a week from Saturday, if that's all right with you. Thought we'd take you up on that weekend in the country offer."

"Sure, that would be great! I'd love to have you. We've had beautiful weather this past week, and I'm sure Ruthie and Penny would be thrilled to see you, too."

"Penny?"

"Oh, you haven't met Penny. She's the newest member of my little family. Ruthie and I took her in when she showed up on my doorstep one evening without so much as a tag or collar."

"Great. The more the merrier. How about we arrive Friday next around four o'clock?"

"Sounds good, we can have a cookout on the back porch."

"Hey, Sis, I found out why your new boyfriend's name sounded so familiar to me. His name was in the paper. Turns out he's an investor in a company called Trade Industries and has been soliciting support from his clients as well. Does that mean anything to you?"

"Yes, funny you should mention it. Trade Industries is looking to acquire land out here to build something, maybe a big housing development. Brent mentioned the name once, but never indicated his connections with them. No wonder he was trying to convince me to sell my place."

"Oh, so how did he take it when you refused?"

"Not well, but he didn't act too concerned about it. I think he was too annoyed because I broke up with him over Ruthie and Penny."

Cliff's laughter filled her ear through the phone. "Guess he didn't know what he was in for when he decided to take you on huh, Sis."

"No, I don't think he did." Clarissa smiled as she envisioned Brent tumbling into the lake the day of their last date.

"Okay, I have to get back to work so I'll see you soon. Bye."

"Yeah, see you soon, Cliff." She replaced the phone back in the cradle.

A phone call and a crank note were an inconvenience at this point, nothing more. She would tell Cliff eventually, if things got worse.

Clarissa went to town and came back with the wire-tapping equipment from the phone company. She followed the instructions, set up everything, and then went to fix supper. The phone didn't ring all evening, but the next day as she started her billing work, it rang.

"Hello?" She listened for a response.

Only heavy breathing sounded on the other end of the line. She pushed the trace button as the phone customer representative had instructed her to do and tried to keep the caller on the line.

"Who is this? What do you want from me? Why are you calling?"

The heavy breathing continued.

After a less than a minute, a disconnect sounded. Well, it might not have been long enough to trace the call, but at least she knew what to do if that person called back.

She called David and Jimmy to invite them over to the cookout Friday next week. She asked Jimmy to bring his family with him, including Booker their basset hound, to meet Penny. She could introduce them to her brother and his girlfriend. Besides, the cookout was the least she could do since they weren't charging her for putting up the electric fence. They both accepted her invitation.

* * * *

Saturday morning, Jimmy and David arrived at ten, as promised, to install the electric fence. They worked hard in the rising sun, and David removed his shirt to cool down. Clarissa felt her own temperature rise as she admired his toned muscles and tan. She really wasn't prepared for the rush of emotion that washed over her as she studied him.

David glanced her way, and she met his gaze with a longing and passion that stirred her. Self-conscious, she turned and went inside to fix them some sandwiches, cookies, and lemonade for lunch.

Returning with a tray full of food, she looked to Jimmy, knowing he wouldn't make her blush the way David did. "How's it going?"

"It's coming along. We'll be done in another hour or two at the most. It's a good thing you have an existing fence to work with or it would take a lot longer to install." Jimmy surveyed their finished work and the ground left to cover. He wiped the sweat from his forehead with an old red bandana he pulled from his pocket.

"Well, I made you both some lunch. You should take at least a thirty-minute break. You've earned it." She set a tray with sandwiches and cookies down on a small table and poured each of them a tall glass of icy lemonade.

Ruthie rubbed up against David's leg and Penny found her way over to Jimmy.

David laughed and reached down to rub Ruthie's ears and side. "Hey there, girl, how are you doing today?" Ruthie responded with a grunt that made everyone laugh.

Jimmy stroked Penny. "You're such a cute little thing. My Booker would surely fall for you."

David smiled and grabbed a sandwich. "Thanks for the lunch. You won't have to worry anymore about the coyotes after today."

"I hope not. Ruthie had a real fright that day and so did I."

Clarissa clenched her hands as she relived the terrifying ordeal. If David hadn't come, she might have lost... No, she would have figured something out. No way would she ever let anything happen to Ruthie.

"Did you know Brent was an investor in a company called Trade Industries?" Clarissa threw this tidbit of information out, hoping to measure some sort of reaction.

"Funny you should mention them," David responded with avid interest. "I had a call offering to buy my property about a week ago. I didn't know Brent had anything to do with them."

"Yeah, well, Brent's one of their investors, and he tried to talk me into moving in with him and selling my place."

David raised his eyebrows. "So, what did you do?"

"I dumped him in the lake, of course."

Clarissa laughed so hard her sides hurt and tears ran down her face. David looked confused.

"It didn't happen quite that way. We went fishing, and I saw a spider in our boat. I panicked and tipped us over. He was furious and dripping wet." She laughed again.

"That is funny. I would have loved to see it." David laughed almost as hard as she had.

"Ruthie didn't like him, and she really sent him packing, or rather I did when I saw how little respect he had for my animals."

"Funny you mention Ruthie running Brent off," Jimmy said. "One of the skunks that hangs around my place ran Donna off the other day when she came calling. Wanted me to sell my place. I told her no way, no how. I think she thought I was going to club her with my hoe 'cause she backed away from me and stepped in a bucket of my garden worms. Then, she fell and landed on a pile of manure and scared the stink out of a nearby skunk. She was fuming mad when she left my place. Get it, *fuming* mad?"

Jimmy laughed along with Clarissa and David. They all were practically crying with tears of laughter.

Clarissa could just envision Donna in her mind and the thought of the incident alone gave her great satisfaction. Miss Prissy Prim and Proper herself.

The two men ate and drank until they were satisfied and prepared to return to work. By the time they finished the eighty feet of electric fence, the thermometer on the front porch showed almost seventy-five degrees.

"You two have done a fine job. I don't know how you managed to finish it so fast. Thank you so much for all your help. You're great neighbors."

She shook hands with Jimmy and then David. David held her hand just a little longer, and Jimmy got a silly look on his face and winked at him. Clarissa blushed and looked away.

"We are happy to help, ma'am," Jimmy responded, a broad smile on his face.

Clarissa waved at them as the two drove off in David's truck. She felt blessed to have friends like them who would help her because they cared for their neighbors. She would find a way to have David slip Jimmy some money for his trouble. Ellen was a good wife, but even she needed cash to pay for the few essentials a family couldn't live without. Clarissa didn't have money to waste considering the price for the fencing, but even twenty or thirty dollars could help ease Jimmy and his family's hardship.

Her hand still tingled where David had held it. This wouldn't do, it wouldn't do at all.

Chapter Nineteen
~ The Cookout ~

That week, two more notes appeared and two phone calls arrived, but Clarissa hadn't succeeded with the phone trace, and her frustration with the caller mounted. She convinced herself the idiot would eventually either tire of the game or leave a clue. It made her angry to think someone was annoying her. Good thing she took a self-defense class when she first moved out here. The caller better hope they never met face to face.

The following Friday at four, her brother Cliff and Mieko arrived for their visit.

"Glad you could make it." Clarissa hugged Cliff and then Mieko. "I know the drive can seem a bit long, but the closer you get, the better the scenery becomes."

Meiko smiled with demure graciousness. "Yes, the scenery is lovely away from the city. Thanks so much for inviting us to join you for the weekend."

"It's good to see you again, Sis." Cliff patted her back.

"Come, I'll show you to the guest room. I have it all ready for you." Clarissa led her brother and his girlfriend to the spare room just off the kitchen.

She had decorated it Oriental style. Large Japanese-style fans lined the walls in addition to paintings of women in kimonos. A black lacquered wooden bed and side tables with intricate details of cherry blossoms inlaid in the wood provided an Oriental flavor to the room, along with the comforter covered with cherry blossom sprays on the bed.

Mieko clasped her hands together. Clarissa noticed a beautiful diamond ring shone bright on her left hand.

"It's beautiful," Mieko exclaimed as she looked around at the décor and at the two Japanese-style robes with slippers on the bed. "You didn't do all this just for me, did you?"

"Actually, I've always admired the Japanese culture, and since I can't go there because of the expense, I thought I would enjoy it this way. I swear one day I'll hire a Japanese decorator to do my whole house."

Clarissa beamed with pride. It was wonderful to see Mieko so happy.

"So, when is the big day?"

Mieko blushed as she looked over at Cliff.

"Valentine's Day," Cliff said, beaming. "We wanted to give ourselves enough time to prepare. We're also hoping to make arrangements for Mieko's parents to join us from Tokyo. It would mean a lot to her if we could fly them in for the wedding."

Cliff looked happier than Clarissa had ever seen him, standing there with his arm around his future wife. She envied them both.

"Congratulations. I'm so happy for you two. You make such a perfect couple. Make yourselves at home. I'll let you get settled and then show you around the place a bit, and we'll start the barbeque. Come out on the porch when you're ready, and I'll introduce you to Ruthie and Penny."

Clarissa left them to settle in while she went to fire up the charcoal grill. She mulled over the idea of her brother being married. When they were growing up, she never thought she'd see the day when Cliff would become mature enough to settle down. Tears of joy came to her eyes as she thought of how happy the couple looked together.

The noise of cars approaching drew her attention. As Jimmy, his family, and David arrived, she walked out to the driveway to greet them.

"Your timing is perfect. I just lit the grill. I thought we could sit on the porch and enjoy the view while we talk." She ushered them toward the porch where Cliff and Mieko waited.

"This is my brother Cliff and his fiancé Mieko. They're here for a weekend country getaway."

"Nice to meet you." David shook hands with Cliff and then Mieko.

"I've heard you're an experienced real estate man and a great brother."

"Yeah, I dabble in some real estate, and as for being a good brother, Sis is biased." Cliff laughed.

"It's really nice of you to invite us all to your cookout, Clarissa," Jimmy said.

"Yes, thank you, Clarissa," Ellen added. "We don't get to take these wild Indians many places." She looked over at her kids with a big smile on her face.

"It's the least I can do since Jimmy and David put up my electric fence."

"We were glad to do it." David smiled at her.

Clarissa felt her face grow warm. She hoped they would think it was in response to lighting the grill.

"I now have peace of mind when I let Ruthie and Penny out in the yard to play. I don't know what I would have done if anything had happened to either one of them." Clarissa reached down to rub Ruthie's ears.

They all took seats on chairs Clarissa had set out on the porch for company. Then, she went inside and returned with platters of raw hamburgers and hot dogs.

"Who would like to be the designated cook?"

"I will," Jimmy volunteered. "I'm a great cook. I'll grill the burgers to perfection." He gave Clarissa a sly smile.

"Okay, Jimmy, here you go." She set the tray on a small table next to the grill.

"Don't worry, Ruthie, they're all beef hotdogs. Sorry Penny, I meant frankfurters." She patted Ruthie and then Penny on the head.

"You'll have to watch the animals. They're very resourceful when it comes to food," she cautioned and sat down in one of the chairs.

"This must be your new addition."

Ellen reached down to pat Penny, and the kids gathered around with their basset hound, Booker. Penny had all four feet in the air and her tail swept the porch, enjoying the belly rub.

"Aw, she's so cute," Julie, Jimmy's daughter, said as she rubbed Penny's tummy.

Clarissa smiled down at Julie. "I'm sure Penny would love to play with all of you and Booker too. Go ahead into the yard and call her name. She'll follow you."

The beautiful little girl made Clarissa think about having her own child one day. She glanced over at David. Their eyes locked for a brief moment, and her heart beat faster.

The kids took Penny and Booker into the yard to play ball. Ruthie followed at their heels while Jasper strolled over to patrol the yard.

"Isn't that a wonderful sight?" David said as he watched the kids playing. "You're a lucky man, Jimmy. A good-looking wife, three beautiful kids, and all of them love you. That's what life's all about."

"Thanks, Doc. I feel like a millionaire sometimes." Jimmy glanced over at Ellen. She smiled back and kissed him. "Don't worry, I left a few good women out there."

He and David both glanced at Clarissa. She blushed red as a peony. David walked over and joined the kids for a game of tag.

There went a man worth ten of Brent. Unselfish, caring, he placed more value on life than money. Why did he have to be her client? If only she didn't have to work with him on a professional level, she would jump at the chance to be with him. He clearly wanted the same things in life she did, and they weren't material possessions.

Jimmy smiled at Clarissa. "There goes a man worth catching."

Clarissa started, certain he was reading her mind.

"He has a good heart. He'll make some lucky woman very happy indeed."

"Yes, he's something else, isn't he?" Clarissa watched David with the kids and the animals.

The kids tossed the ball around to each other and then rolled the ball toward Ruthie and she rolled it to Penny. Penny tried to chew the ball until Booker stole it from her. Jasper sat and watched the whole thing from the sidelines. He twitched his tail each time the ball came near him and prepared to pounce. When the ball finally made its way around to David, he picked it up and tossed it to Tommy, Jimmy's oldest son. After about five or ten minutes, David had to stop to catch his breath.

"It's okay, Dr. Claremont, you can sit this next game out if you're tired," Tommy reassured him.

"Thanks, Tommy, I think I will. I'm not as young or as fit as I wish."

David took a seat on the porch steps where he proceeded to rub Ruthie, Penny, and Jasper who had decided to take a break from playing games, too. Ruthie snorted with pleasure while Penny just licked David's hand. Jasper walked around the porch railing and settled down where he could watch Jimmy cook the food.

Clarissa could almost feel those strong fingers on her skin. *Stop that*, she admonished herself. So, this man was good with animals and kids. So what? Something told her Brent wouldn't have joined in the games. She had been so physically attracted to him that she had blinded herself to his imperfections. David had all the qualities Brent lacked. She banished thoughts of Brent from her mind.

The kids played until called to eat, and then they all chose hotdogs over hamburgers. Most of the adults had cheeseburgers, and the men ate both. The adults liked the potato salad Clarissa had made, and the kids filled up on potato chips. For dessert, she served Heavenly Hash.

"You can fix this anytime for me," David said and took another spoonful of dessert.

"Me, too," added young Jimmie.

Clarissa laughed. "Tell you what, I'll give the recipe to your mother, and she can make it for you at home."

"Okay, that'll be great!" Little Jimmy looked as if he had found gold in his backyard. "What about the doc?"

"Oh, don't worry about the doctor; I'll fix him some anytime he wants. After all, he is my next-door neighbor."

Clarissa smiled at David and he grinned back. It almost felt for a moment as if they were the only two in the universe as their eyes locked. *Get control of yourself*, she scolded.

The evening flew by as the adults talked and snacked while the kids resumed playing with the animals. Cliff and David carried on an animated conversation while Mieko and Ellen chatted like old friends. Clarissa and Jimmy talked about the wild animals in the area and how the fence would help keep her pets safe. By the time the women cleared the remains of the feast, the sun was setting.

"Thank you all for coming," Clarissa said. "It was a pleasure having you."

"We had a wonderful time," Ellen said.

She shook hands with Clarissa, waved to Mieko, and then headed with the yawning kids for the old Buick followed by Jimmy. David waved as he left, with Jasper following right behind him.

Clarissa returned to the porch where Cliff waited. Mieko had turned in for the night.

"You should consider getting together with that one." Cliff looked toward David's truck as it drove away. "I like him, and he certainly likes you."

"What makes you say that?" Clarissa looked at her brother with suspicion.

"'Because he talks a lot about you, and he worries about you."

"He's a great guy, but he's a client." Clarissa gazed at her feet, unwilling to face Cliff.

"Yeah, so? What difference does that make?"

"Well, I don't date my clients." Clarissa frowned and crossed her arms.

"Just an observation. You don't have to get yourself worked up over it." He grinned at her.

"It's okay. I know you mean well, and he is a pretty great guy, but I'm not ready to take it any further than that." She hoped that would satisfy him.

David attracted her so much that she really had to work hard at restraining herself. Her body reacted to him, while her head told her to get a grip on herself. Maybe one day she would give in and throw caution to the wind, but now didn't seem like the right time.

* * * *

Clarissa showed Cliff and Mieko around her house on Saturday and took them on a walking tour of the property. She walked them to the end of the property lines and to where David's began. Jasper joined them for part of the tour, and Cliff really took a liking to him.

"Aren't you a good-looking cat?" Cliff stroked him from head to tail, rubbing the fluffy orange fur. "I bet your master loves you."

"Yes, David's very fond of Jasper, and so am I. He often comes to visit Ruthie and Penny." Clarissa looked down at the purring cat.

When they returned from the hike, the red flag was up on the mailbox.

"That's funny. That flag wasn't up before we left."

Cliff opened the box before she could and read the note aloud. "I'll be waiting."

It looked just like the others, using pasted newspaper clippings.

"What does this mean?" He held out the note for Clarissa to see.

"Oh, um…some jerk likes playing games. It's nothing serious, mostly silly notes." She crumpled the note in a tight fist.

"Don't you think you should report this?" Cliff frowned.

"I already did. The police say they can't do anything with the notes 'cause they're not handwritten. As for the calls…" She clamped her hand over her mouth.

Damn! Why did she open her big mouth? Now he would worry even more.

"So you're getting phone calls, too?" He raised an eyebrow. "What does this caller say?"

"Nothing, he just breathes like a bad imitation of Darth Vader."

Cliff laughed at her comparison, but then turned to her with a serious look on his face. "You tell them the next time he calls that you have a brother who will gladly come out and kick his ass. Tell them I'm looking forward to that."

"'I will, but don't worry, I have everything under control. See, the local electronics store in town provided me with that tracing equipment."

She directed his attention to the elaborate phone setup. Clarissa patted his arm to reassure him.

"Just the same, you call me if you need me. I don't want anything to happen to my only sister." He hugged her tight.

The subject was dropped for the remainder of the visit. Cliff and Mieko enjoyed spending time on the back porch with Clarissa, watching the animals play as the sun set.

"Is it always this beautiful out here?" Mieko asked.

"Always, That's why I moved out here." Clarissa smiled over at her.

Mieko gave her an understanding glance.

* * * *

161

Sunday morning, Cliff and Mieko thanked her for a wonderful time and agreed to come for another visit in the future. Clarissa waved to them as they drove down the drive. She still had no clue to the note and caller. She wondered what kind of deranged person with too much time on their hands would want to mess with her, and why.

Chapter Twenty
~ The Intruder ~

The strange notes and calls continued for several weeks, but declined in frequency. She started to think of it as a silly game, so she stopped reporting the incidences and ignored them. David assured her he would keep an eye out for her and to call him if anything happened and she needed someone to come right away.

Relieved her life had settled down since the break with Brent, Clarissa began to think about dating again. Yet somehow, she couldn't bring herself to commit to a serious relationship. With no candidates in sight, it was a moot issue. Besides, finding someone took too much time, and she had a lot of work to do.

Meeting with David every week for lunch on Mondays and the occasional concert or public event like a town festival provided her with enough human interaction to satisfy her. Besides, she found David funny and entertaining. They continued their lunch dates and their occasional outings, and her affectionate respect for him grew despite her resistance.

One day at lunch, David faced her across their usual table at Café Corner. "You know, I wonder if those calls could have anything to do with the Trade Industries deal going sour."

"What? Trade Industries left town? Where did you hear that?" Clarissa's eyes grew wide with surprise.

"It was in the newspaper just the other day. I hear Brent lost a lot of money on his investment in the housing complex they wanted to build on our land. Perhaps he or someone else wants revenge?"

Worry lines covered David's forehead. He placed his warm hands on top of hers.

"Umm, guess that's why the orange flags disappeared. No one around here is willing to sell their land."

Clarissa blushed with the warmth from David's hands. She struggled to concentrate on the conversation and not the sudden rise in her body temperature.

Why would Trade Industries have any interest in her and not David or Jimmy? It made no sense.

"No, David, that company is huge and makes plenty more good deals than bad ones. Why would this deal be more important than any other? Besides, Brent couldn't be that type of person. He might be annoyed, but he never struck me as the stalking type."

"Anyway, I'm still keeping an eye on you. I wouldn't want anything to happen to you. You're an excellent biller, but first and foremost, you're my neighbor and best friend." He gazed into her eyes with concern and candor.

Best friend? That gave her a thrill, but also brought her down to earth. Friends didn't desire one another.

"You mean a great deal to me, too, but I'll be fine. Let's enjoy our lunch and talk about the town festival this weekend. I hope you can go with me."

She didn't think that would be out of line for a friend. It wasn't much different from him asking her to a concert.

"I wouldn't miss it for the world. Besides, if you don't take me, Donna might pounce on me, and we can't have that, can we?"

"No, definitely not. I wouldn't wish her on you or any other nice man. Well, maybe one other man. She and Brent would be perfect together, both scheming to take a leprechaun hostage for his pot of gold." She laughed and David joined her.

Lunch had been as pleasant as always, but something about this particular lunch nagged at her. She thought about all the time she and David had spent together since they first met. Images like a movie filled her mind. She could see the look on his face when she had shoved her welcome fruit basket into his hands and all the times he flashed that brilliant smile of his at her. Those loving looks, his laughter, the gentle touches and words, it was as if some barrier she had constructed between David and herself had been broken.

Somehow, he now seemed a lot less like a client and much more like a man she wanted in her life and in her bed. Her resistance was diminishing like those Russian nesting dolls that got smaller as you opened each one. The funny thing was that she didn't care anymore. She had been fighting against her feelings for so long that she had started to forget why she was resisting. She went home to Ruthie and Penny who greeted her with joyful abandon, anxious for their walk.

* * * *

The weekend arrived before Clarissa realized it, and David came to pick her up in his truck. They arrived in town with the festival in full swing. The police had closed Main Street to traffic. Rides and games with prizes instead of parked cars lined it. Stands sold cotton candy and candy apples, two of Clarissa's favorite childhood carnival treats.

"Wow, this town really goes all out for their festivals. I wouldn't have expected so much from a small place." David stared at all the activity with surprise.

"Yeah, we country folks love our festivities. It gives us all a chance to socialize and let off steam after working hard week after week. Let's take a ride on the Ferris wheel." Clarissa led him to her favorite ride. When they reached the top, she gripped the safety bar tight.

"Here, let me keep you safe."

David put his arm around her, and she instinctively hugged him, hiding her face in his jacket as the movement from the carriage spooked her.

"I take it you're afraid of heights?"

"A little afraid, but I love the view of the town from up here and the thrill it gives me." Clarissa loosened her grip on him a little.

David looked out. "Wow, it is a pretty amazing view from up here. I'm glad I let you talk me into this."

After leaving the ride, they strolled down the street enjoying the night air. When they approached the candy apple concession, they saw Donna with Brent.

Donna waved to them. "Clarissa, David, what a nice surprise." She spoke as if they were all best friends. The self-satisfied gleam in her eyes annoyed Clarissa.

Placing her hand on Brent's arm, Donna gave him a coy smiled. "I hope you don't mind, but Brent and I are dating now."

"No hard feelings, right, Clarissa?" Brent looked at her with a raised eyebrow followed by a faint scowl.

"No, not at all, congratulations." She smiled at the two.

Then, a momentary twinge of jealousy struck Clarissa. She blinked, taken by surprise. Why would she be jealous? It's wasn't as if she wanted Brent. No way, after having seen what he did to her animals. His good looks had fooled her. That and the sexual aura he exuded. She suspected that probably had the same effect on many women as Donna had said.

"I'm so glad. Well, we'll see you around. Brent is taking me on the Farris wheel next." Donna and Brent walked off with arms around each other.

"You have to give them credit for being the perfect couple," David observed. "They both enjoy the pursuit of money, lots of money. I just wonder who the bigger gold digger is." David and Clarissa laughed together.

They played some games and took more rides. David ate a candy apple and Clarissa a cone of cotton candy. By the end of the night, exhaustion took its toll, and she needed a good night's sleep. David looked zapped too.

"Shall we call it a night?"

He yawned. "Sounds great to me. I'll get the truck and take you home."

He soon returned with the vehicle and held the door open for Clarissa. It felt like an electric spark jumped when he took her hand. Neither of them said much on the drive home. He stopped in the driveway and hurried around to open the truck door for her.

"I had a really great time," she said to David as he walked her to her house.

"Me, too. Thanks for inviting me." He leaned in close and the faint sense of his aftershave reached her.

Clarissa, sensitive to his signals and anxious to stop anything more, gave him a quick kiss that left him no time to react. "Good night, see you tomorrow."

She slipped inside before he could even say a word and closed the door. She hoped he experienced the same elation as she had over the kiss. She waited for him to go. The sound of his truck leaving her driveway reassured her. She could still feel his warm, smooth lips touching hers as she changed for bed.

"What am I going to do about that man?" she said to Ruthie and Penny as she climbed into bed. "I really like him, and part of me wants to be with him, but the other part tells me it's wrong. Everyone says he's perfect for me. I guess I know they're right, but that only makes it harder. Best to sleep on it and let nature take whatever course it will." She patted Ruthie and Penny and rolled over in her bed.

Images of David with her at the coffee shop, at the concert, at the carnival, laughing together on her front porch filled her dreams. Every time they were together she saw a ring on his finger, but she couldn't see her hands. What did it mean?

Did he marry someone else in the future? The dream ended with David driving away with a beautiful redhead as Clarissa stood waving good-bye. She woke up crying and feeling as if she'd lost her best friend. In that moment, she realized she loved David. Did he feel the same way about her? All the times they'd been together, he treated her like a queen and looked at her like...like a man in love.

Kaboom! The sound of thunder startled her and she looked down at her animals.

Ruthie and Penny slept in their beds, with soft snorts from Ruthie now and then, and Penny twitching a bit. Clarissa tossed, unable to settle back to sleep because of the thunderstorm and thoughts of the carnival.

Damn David! Why did the one man she regarded as off-limits attract her so much?

With a small snort, almost a question, Ruthie sat up, ears perked. Alerted, Penny followed suit with a low growl.

Thump, thump.

The noise frightened Clarissa. Now what? Surely, the coyotes wouldn't come near the house or nose around the back porch. The noise came again.

Someone or something rummaged around on the back porch. Clarissa grabbed the comforter about her. Disoriented, she reached for an umbrella she kept handy.

Kaboom!

Another flash of lightening lit up the room. She hated guns, but an umbrella provided a great weapon. It had a pointed end, and she could flap it at any intruder. Armed, she moved to the door of her bedroom, followed by Ruthie and Penny.

A sound came from the kitchen like someone walking around, but stumbling in the dark. Ruthie streaked forward and brushed past Clarissa. Penny padded after.

Clarissa switched on the night-light next to her bed. She pulled on her robe, slid her feet into her slippers, and eased the door open. She poked her head out, listening.

Kaboom!

Lightening lit the room, illuminating a figure in black crossing the living room and coming toward her. She screamed.

Ruthie ran straight at the thing, squealing for all she was worth. Penny came tearing through the kitchen barking as loud as she could. Ruthie grabbed one ankle and Penny the other.

A yowl of pain came from the stranger who whirled around in circles and shook both legs, one after the other, to dislodge Ruthie and Penny. Her two pets hung tight, refusing to turn the villain loose.

"Let go," a deep voice shouted. "Damn you, let go." The leg kicked out at Ruthie, but she hung tight. Penny's growl grew louder.

Why was this person in her house? Was this the same one leaving the notes and making the phone calls? Were they mad because she had been ignoring the notes and calls and decided to pay her a visit? She couldn't think of who or why someone would be bothering her.

Desperate to reach help, Clarissa ran for her room and locked the door behind her. With shaking fingers, she dialed 911. "I have an intruder at 3453 Monet Road. Come quick."

Ruthie squealed in ear-splitting screams. "He's killing Ruthie!"

Chapter Twenty-One
~ Love is Revealed ~

Jasper jumped into David's lap as he held a diamond ring in his hands. He was thinking about the perfect proposal, but Jasper's meowing and clawing distracted him.

"What's wrong, Jazz?" David stroked the disturbed cat. Jasper jumped down and ran through the pet door and then raced back, digging his sharp claws into David's arm.

"Ouch!" Alarmed, David jumped to his feet and grabbed his shotgun. "What's up, Jasper?"

Was there another coyote problem? Had something happened to Clarissa? Once outside, he heard Ruthie squealing at the top of her lungs while Penny howled. Thunder sounded in the distance as he raced to his truck and jerked the door open. Jasper jumped in, too. David slid in behind the wheel and put the shotgun in the built-in rack behind his seat. The engine started with a roar.

He had to reach Clarissa before something bad occurred. His intense concern for her made him realize with undeniable clarity he was in love with the woman. If anyone hurt her, he'd kill them.

David raised a cloud of dust as he slammed on his brakes and jumped out in Clarissa's driveway. Using the moonlight and the spare key Clarissa had given him after the coyote incident, he opened the front door. With shotgun in hand and Jasper right by his side, David raced through the house. He followed the noise to a commotion in the bathroom.

"You've bitten off more than you can chew this time, mister!" Clarissa yelled at a figure dressed in black, all the while opening and

169

closing her big umbrella and jabbing it at him.

Black-covered legs dangled half in and half out of the bathroom window as a dark-clothed person struggled to escape. Ruthie clung tight to one ankle and Penny the other as the intruder hollered in pain.

Jasper came running into the bathroom and leaped into the air, claws extended, latching onto the intruder's back. A loud howl followed as Jasper sunk his claws and teeth into flesh.

"Eeeooowww!" The man howled again and squeezed the rest of the way through the window with one cat firmly attached.

David's first reaction was to burst out laughing. It had to be one of the funniest sights he'd ever seen.

"You okay, Clarissa?"

She nodded, dropping the large umbrella and struggling to catch her breath.

David headed to the front of the house where he turned on the porch light. He dashed outside and around the side of the house with his shotgun ready. Sirens sounded off in the distance, growing closer. The intruder stood below the window struggling to dislodge the determined Jasper.

"Hold it right there, buddy. You and I are going to wait for the police to arrive." David aimed his shotgun with deadly accuracy at the man's stomach. "If you move, my trigger finger here might just slip, and instead of a jail cell, you'll be visiting the morgue."

As two police cars pulled up, one officer yanked out a pair of handcuffs to secure the masked perpetrator's arms behind his back. David lowered his shotgun.

As the cop cuffed the masked intruder, another recited his rights. "You have the right to remain silent. Anything you say can and will be used against you in a court of law…" The dark-haired officer continued reading the intruder his rights.

"Radio the station, Ben. Tell them we have our suspect in custody and are bringing him in," he told his partner.

* * * *

"Oh, thank God you got him." Relief washed over Clarissa as she joined David on the front lawn with the animals. "He broke in through

170

my back door. You can see the broken window he used to reach in and unlock the door. He must have used the storm to cover up the sound of breaking glass."

"Yes ma'am, I believe you're right. We have him in custody now. Maybe you can identify him for us." The officer pulled the ski mask off the trespasser.

Clarissa stared for a moment and then shook her head. "No, I've never seen this man in my life."

She stared at culprit in bewilderment. Then she thought of the phone calls and the notes.

"You phoned and sent the notes, didn't you? Why? "

The young man glared at her.

"You're Donna Gilead's handyman," David shouted as he recognized the scar on the man's left cheek. "Did she put you up to this?"

"Yeah, well, she paid me good money. Said I'd get more if I succeeded in scaring the owner into moving." The man scowled as the police led him to the squad car.

"We'll need you to come by the station tomorrow, ma'am, if we are to keep him and prosecute him," the first officer informed her as he loaded the man into the car and shut the door. "With his confession, you can also press charges against Ms. Gilead."

"Yes, no problem," Clarissa nodded. "I understand. I'll be there first thing in the morning." David put his arm around her as she wavered, unsteady on her feet.

"Guess you won't have to worry about this one anymore. You can relax now and sleep better at night knowing he's in jail." The police officer waved his hand as he got in his car and drove away.

Clarissa looked to David. "I'm so glad you were here. I was scared to death. How did you know?"

"Jasper alerted me. He kept running around like crazy and jumping on me to get my attention. When I went outside, I heard Ruthie and Penny. Great watch animals you have there."

"You're so right, but I was afraid the man would hurt them."

"I drove down here as fast as I could only to find you and your girls had things under control. You looked rather menacing with that umbrella in your hand. No, I don't imagine Donna warned her handyman about your animals. She probably thought them harmless. The guy certainly wasn't prepared for Ruthie and Penny, and I don't think he had any idea about Jasper."

David laughed and held his arms out to Clarissa. She laughed and then cried into David's shirt, soaking it with her tears. All her sadness and frustration came pouring out at once and she couldn't contain her feelings anymore. Lately, things had not gone the way she planned. Her thoughts overwhelmed her. Tony her ex, Brent, the coyote scare, the intruder, her overwhelming attraction to David.

Wrapping his arms around her, David held her close and stroked her hair, reassuring her everything was okay. "I love you, Clarissa," he said. "From that first day when you stormed away, leaving me with that welcome basket of fruit. But you fought against us so hard. It was as if I had some kind of disease. Then Brent, the jerk, tried to muscle in on my girl."

He looked into her eyes. "How you could choose him over me I don't know. I'm just glad you came to your senses. Why did you fight against the idea of us for so long anyway?"

"I…I guess I was being stubborn. I hated the fact you hunt, and I didn't want to mix business with pleasure, but you were always there for me being a good neighbor and friend. After that coyote, I sort of changed my mind about the gun thing. Soon after that, I realized you were the one I really wanted, not Brent. The worst of it is, the harder I tried to resist my true feelings for you the more I realized I wanted to be with you. I'm sorry I've been so stubborn."

She looked down at her hands. "I still don't like guns, but I guess they have their place. I fell in love with you, too, David, but didn't want to accept it because you're a client. Then I realized you're my best friend."

She looked up at him seeking his understanding. "I would feel incomplete without you in my life."

David hugged her close and kissed her on the top of her head.

"Besides, Ruthie and Penny have already adopted you." Clarissa laughed along with David. "I love you, David. I don't care if you are my client."

With the tears still streaming down her face, David kissed her. His lips felt perfect on hers, and for once, she didn't turn away. His kiss, sweet and gentle, lit a fire in her that threatened to consume her. Then she broke away to catch her breath.

"Come, I'll show you my castle." She laughed as she reached her hand out to him.

He laughed as well and took her hand. The two of them walked into the house with Ruthie, Penny, and Jasper following behind them. She led David into her bedroom.

* * * *

Sunlight streamed in through the window. Ruthie and Penny tugged at the covers, nudging Clarissa and David awake. Jasper, at the foot of the bed, stretched and yawned. The animals seemed to know morning sunshine meant breakfast.

Clarissa looked over at David who still appeared to be sleeping peacefully. As she began to crawl out of bed, trying not to wake him, he grabbed her around the waist and pulled her close. His kiss consumed her with the same fiery passion she felt the night before. She had lost count of how many times they'd made love in her large, comfortable bed.

"Good morning, darling…I love you." David told her.

"I love you, too, David. I always will." Telling him her true feelings removed a terrible burden from her. No more hiding how she felt about him.

He rolled her onto her back and slowly made love to her, kissing her, and reminding her that last night was real. She floated above the clouds and when it ended, she had to force herself back to earth.

Ruthie, Penny, and Jasper made noises. They considered it past time for breakfast.

"Okay, you three, we get the hint. I'm coming."

Clarissa patted Ruthie on her nose as she slid on her slippers and headed for the kitchen. David slowly rousted himself out of bed to follow. After letting the girls and Jasper out into the yard, she completed her own morning routine. She prepared breakfast for David, her, and the animals, opening a can of tuna fish for Jasper.

As the two of them sat down to breakfast in the kitchen, David acted like he was up to something with his facial expressions similar to that of a child trying to keep a secret.

"Why don't you call our animals in here—I have an announcement to make before we take our first shower together."

David smiled as if he had won the lottery. After a night and morning of passionate lovemaking such as she had never known, Clarissa couldn't imagine anything better.

"Ruthie, come here, baby. Penny, Jasper, here kitty, kitty." The animals all came running and sat down next to one another, anxiously awaiting an expected treat. "You're up to something." She frowned.

David got down on the floor on one knee and pulled a small black box out from his pocket. Clarissa drew in a deep breath as she realized what he intended.

"Clarissa Wilford, I love you. I have never loved another woman in my life. We are true soul mates, and I don't want to go another day without asking you to marry me. Will you be my wife?" He looked at her with more love than she'd ever seen in any man's eyes.

With one little word, she changed both their lives forever.

"Yes. Absolutely and positively *yes!* I would be honored to marry you and become your wife. You've made my life complete in so many ways."

She embraced him, and they hugged like they would never be together again. Clarissa felt joy flowing through her body like a river, and she knew they would grow old together.

A vision of her walking down the aisle at her wedding and a tall, dark-haired groom came to mind. In her dream, the groom was never revealed. Now she knew with certainty it had never been Brent. It was always David.

Epilogue
~ Three Years Later ~

Clarissa smiled as she watched the little tricolored basset puppies running around in the yard. Penny sat watching over her young. Ruthie stood, rubbing her head on Clarissa's leg with Jasper on her other side.

A little girl of two with green eyes and rosy cheeks held her arms up toward her father. "Up Daddy, up Daddy."

David reached down and picked his daughter Susan up in his arms. He kissed her on the forehead. "I love you, sweetheart. You're my little princess."

"I love you, too, Daddy," Susan said. She squirmed to be let down.

David set her down, and she ran to play with Penny's puppies.

Just then, Jimmy and his family pulled up in the driveway.

"Hey there, everyone, I have some good news about the puppies. I found homes for almost all of them." Jimmy waved to David and Clarissa.

"Sounds great." David smiled as he put his arm around Clarissa and kissed her.

"Thank you so much for helping to find homes for them." Clarissa watched her daughter Susan playing with Jimmy's kids and the pups.

"I feel sorta' responsible since it was my dog Booker that got Penny pregnant in the first place. Guess I didn't keep a close enough eye on him at all your cookouts." He laughed along with David and Clarissa.

"How are you holding up?" Ellen asked Clarissa indicating her growing belly.

"Pretty good so far, although I hope I don't get any bigger. I think it's a boy."

"Oh, why is that?"

"Because he sure kicks me a lot and moves around much more than Susan did."

"Well, we just wanted to stop by and give you the good news about the pups. I knew it would make your day." Ellen patted Clarissa's stomach. "He does seem to want out of there."

"Any idea what you're going to do with the runt?" Jimmy said.

"I think we're going to keep that one. Susan has already named it and fallen in love with it. It would break her little heart if we sold it." Clarissa looked over at her daughter and smiled.

"What did she name it?"

"Donna," Clarissa replied.

Jimmy laughed and soon all the adults were laughing. Booker and Penny were touching noses.

"Sorry, Booker, Penny is getting fixed. There'll be no more making babies for you two," David hollered to the dogs.

The two of them just looked over at him and went back to their Eskimo kisses.

Later, after Jimmy and his family had gone home, David took Clarissa in his arms.

"Our fourth-year anniversary is coming up soon. It's hard to believe it's been that long. It seems like yesterday when my wife called me rude and obnoxious and left me standing on my front porch with a welcome basket in my hands. I'm so glad you changed your mind about me. I couldn't imagine life without you." David stood there with a smile of joy on his face.

Clarissa leaned over with her large belly protruding and kissed her husband on the lips. "So, Mr. Claremont, have all your dreams come true?" She smiled at him, her eyes twinkling like diamonds.

"Why yes, Mrs. Claremont, I believe they have, right down to the little girl from the painting in my living room and my own personal hunting cabin."

He kissed her and pulled her close to hold her. Susan joined them, and David scooped her up. Now he had both his girls.

Penny barked up at them from their feet, and Ruthie snorted while Jasper just circled around their legs.

"We love you, too, girls. You, too, Jasper. You know you're part of the family." Clarissa laughed. At last, she had love and the family she always wanted.

THE END

About the Author

Tenaya E. Jacob was born in Sydney, Australia where she grew up until the age of seven. She moved to Columbus, OH where as a teenager and young adult she wrote many poems, which were published in "Seasonings of the Soul". She is married and has two adult children, a granddaughter and several stepchildren. Tenaya lives in southeastern Ohio with her husband and enjoys spending time with her family and friends. She has a bachelor degree in healthcare and does web design and writing during her spare time. "For the Love of Ruthie" is Tenaya's first romance novel and she is now working on a paranormal romantic suspense. She has other publications, which include her poetry and children's stories.

https://www.facebook.com/tenaya.jacob ,
http://www.freewebs.com/teb569/